JESSIE KESSON

was born Jessie Grant McDonald in Inverness in 1915, and soon moved to Elgin with her beloved mother (she never knew her father). Estranged from many of the family, mother and daughter were forced to live off their own resources, and Jessie's early days were spent dodging the Cruelty Inspector and the rent man, before she was sent to an orphanage in Skene, Aberdeenshire. As a teenager, she entered service, settling in 1934 on a farm with her husband Johnnie, a cottar. Those early years have inspired much of her work: the novels, *The White Bird Passes* (1958), *Glitter of Mica* (1963) and *Another Time, Another Place* (1983, also published by Virago), as well as short stories such as *Where the Apple Ripens* (1985). *The White Bird Passes* and *Another Time, Another Place* were prize-winning films in 1980 and 1983 respectively.

Until recently, whether she was writing stories, poems, newspaper features, dramas or novels, Jessie Kesson has always done other jobs. She has been a cinema cleaner, an artists' model and was, for nearly twenty years, a social worker in London and Glasgow. Now a great-grandmother, and the proud owner of a 'scarlet goon' (conferred by Dundee University in 1984), she lives with Johnnie in London, where she is currently writing the story of her remarkable life and a dramatisation of *Glitter of Mica*.

Glitter of Mica and *Where the Apple Ripens* will be published by Virago in 1993.

VIRAGO
MODERN
CLASSIC
NUMBER
378

Jessie Kesson

THE
WHITE BIRD
PASSES

Bright is the ring of words
When the right man rings them
And the maid remembers.

R.L.S.

Published by VIRAGO PRESS Limited 1992
20–23 Mandela Street, Camden Town, London NW1 0HQ

First published in Great Britain by Chatto & Windus Ltd., 1958
Copyright © Jessie Kesson 1958
Virago edition offset from The Hogarth Press 1987 edition

The right of Jessie Kesson to be identified as the author of this work
has been asserted by her in accordance with the Copyright, Designs
and Patents Act 1988.

A CIP catalogue record for this book is available from the British Library

Printed in Great Britain by Cox & Wyman Ltd., Reading, Berks.

For
My Dominie, Donald Murray

Chapter One

OUR Lady's Lane; that was what the Monks had called this thoroughfare eight hundred years ago. The name may have fitted it in their time; perhaps it had been a green and cloistered place in those distant days. But, in this Year of Grace 1926, it was no longer green, although it still remained cloistered.

Lady's Lane was a tributary of High Street, one of many such tributaries of long, narrow wynds that slunk backwards from the main street, gathering themselves into themselves, like a group of women assuring each other proudly, "We keep ourselves to ourselves", and, at the same time, usually knowing more than most people of what is going on around.

If you rushed down High Street in a hurry, you wouldn't notice Lady's Lane at all, so narrowly and darkly does it skulk itself away, but Lady's Lane would most certainly see you. At all hours of the day a voluntary look-out lounges against the entrance to the Lane. It may be Poll Pyke, Battleaxe, or the Duchess. For those ladies of the Lane are in some mysterious way self-appointed guardians of the Lane. The Duchess is the supreme guardian of course. Poll Pyke and Battleaxe are merely her faithful henchwomen, competent enough to take over temporary command on these not infrequent occasions when the Duchess is forcibly removed to Barclamp Jail for ten days without the option, and wary enough to step down from office the moment the Duchess's "time" is up.

The less ambitious occupants of the Lane were quite content with this order of things. It meant that they could swipe the bugs from the walls of their sub-lets in peace, in the sure and certain knowledge that, if anything exciting and untoward was taking place in another part of the Lane, they wouldn't miss it; they would receive a clarion call from the Duchess to come and bear witness to such goings on.

Only the children of the Lane were irked by such vigilance. To get up through the Lane unnoticed took on the face of an adventure, and became triumph indeed, if they could reach their own doors without the Duchess confronting them with a pillow-slip, threepence, and a threat: "Run up to Riley's back-door for a stale loaf, tuppence of broken biscuits. And see you that the loaf isna' too stale." Or Annie Frigg trapping them with her tin plate, her persuasive voice, and a promise: "My fine queanie take a runnie down to Lossie Will's for a tanner of herrings. Your legs are younger nor mine. And I've got something for you. A great big ball. All the colours of the rainbow it is. Blue, red, green, and yellow. And there's something else about this ball that I've

8

got. It will never burst. Run on now, for my herrings. That's a queanie!"

And though the Lane's children knew from experience that Annie's promises never came true, they grew up and they grew old before they finally lost their hope that one day Annie Frigg might really give them a ball of all colours that would never burst.

Janie was one of the children who never quite lost faith in Annie.

"Annie Frigg's giving me a doll," she shouted to Gertie Latham, as she struggled up the cobbles with a pail of water. "If I carry her water for her, she's going to give me a doll."

"Some doll," Gertie responded. "Annie Frigg's just an old twister. It's Salac's night, Janie. Let that old bitch carry her own water, and come on. We'll play the Salacs up for a laugh."

"But the doll," Janie said reluctantly, "it's a fairy one."

"What about the toy piano she promised you? and the skipping rope? And all the other things she was going to give you for carrying her water?" Gertie went on relentlessly. "What about all those things?"

"She just couldn't lay hands on them," Janie explained. "She's got them all, Gertie. Some-where in her room, I'm sure she's got them all. She can tell you every bit about what they're like. She couldn't do that if they weren't there at all. Could she, now?"

"O.K." Gertie became resigned to the inevitable. "Be a soft mark if you like. I'm away for my supper. Hurry up out, Janie. It's Salac's night."

Trauchling up Annie's stairs with the pail of water, now almost half empty, Janie recalled her Mother's verdict on Annie: "There's one thing about Annie, she'll never send you away with a sore heart." Nor did she.

"Here's your water, Missis Frigg," Janie shouted, bracing herself against the smell of cats that was going to rush out and catch her breath the instant Annie opened the door. "It was awful heavy that water. I thought I'd never get up here with it." Like Jack in the Box, Annie's head popped round the door, a grey, curly head, like a golliwog grown old, and a mouth that looked as if it had a black moustache above it, but Janie knew it wasn't a moustache, it was just the snuff that Annie took to clear her head.

"My fine queanie. There's no' a better queanie in the Lane." Annie's eyes twinkled, and Janie, a willing prisoner, stood caught again in the spell of Annie's promises. "About that doll you're to get, I've got an idea it might be lying under some bits of things that's come from America. Some bits belonging to my cousin's bairn; just your size she is. And my word there's some bonnie bits that will fit you. There's a blue velvet frock for one thing. And a ribbon to go with it. I'm having a sort out just now. And when I've sorted out, you're the queanie that's going to get the fine surprise, or my name's not Annie Frigg!"

Janie emerged as always, empty handed but full-visioned after an encounter with Annie, and with but one small doubt, how to share the delight of this new promise with Gertie, who could never see that something to look forward to, and something to dream about, were such glad things, even when you knew within yourself that they might never come true.

It was Janie's day to be "caught".

"That you, Janie?" Mysie Walsh's voice called to her from across the landing. "Run a message for me, luv?"

Janie needed no second bidding. Doing something for Mysie Walsh brought its own reward, and it wasn't the threepenny bit she always gave you either. She was big and bright and safe. And next to Janie's own Mother, Janie thought her the loveliest woman in the Lane, with a smile that sucked you right into the core of its warmness, and plump arms that caught you and squeezed you when she was excited, and left your small body trembling with something of her own sudden excitement. Sometimes, with a sudden impulse to please the women grouped round the entrance to the Lane, Mysie Walsh would dance to the music coming from the chip shop's gramophone, her petticoats whirling, her garters showing, real and silk, her voice rising above the gramophone; and, like her smile, her voice gathered you right into it, so that her song seemed to come from you, too:

> *Yes, I'm goin',*
> *Yes, I'm goin',*
> *And soon I'll be hullo-in*
> *That coal black Mammy of Mine!*

In moments like those the Lane became so alive and full of colour to Janie that she felt suddenly and intensely glad for just being alive in a world of song, and colour, and whirling petticoats and warm, dark women like Mysie Walsh.

"What message do you want me to get?" Janie sniffed the room. It smelt, as always, different from all the other rooms in the Lane, of powder and cream and scent, all mixed up together and coming out in one great sweet smell, which Janie thought of as the smell of a woman that's lovely.

"Cheese. A quarter will do, luv."

The request, as much as the tone in which it was requested, aroused Janie from her contemplation of the room. Mysie Walsh lay on the top of her bed, her face hidden in the pillow. Janie had never seen Mysie Walsh without her face, dark and laughing. She sensed there was something wrong.

"Have you been taken ill?" she asked the head on the pillow.

"No. Not ill. You'll find money for the cheese on the mantelpiece, or on the table somewhere."

"You're awfully sad, then?"

"Real sad. Hurry, Janie, or you won't catch McKenzie's open."

"Just cheese? Nothing else?"

"Just cheese. Just a quarter. Shut the door behind you."

Cheese. Not like Mysie Walsh's usual messages, Janie thought to herself, as she ran up High Street. Mysie Walsh's messages were usually as delightful as herself. Phulnana from the chemists, a smell of it, a little on your own cheeks, rubbed well in by Mysie Walsh herself, and the promise of the jar to yourself forever and ever when the cream was done. Or a comb from Woolworth's, the brightest one you could find, with gold stars on it, that shone through Mysie Walsh's hair, even when it was tucked away, and her old comb with only some of the teeth out for yourself. Or cream buns, not stale ones either. "And we'll have one with a cup of tea together when you come back, luvie." All the other people in the Lane bought a quarter of cheese, or polony, or a tin of condensed milk. "And tell McKenzie to mark it on the book." But not Mysie Walsh. You never had to get it marked on the book for her, because amongst all her other enchantments, Mysie Walsh also always had money.

Twenty minutes later Janie stood in the Lane debating what to do with the money in her hand.

Two shillings. The biggest amount she had ever had. More than Mysie Walsh had ever given her before. "Keep the change, Janie," Mysie Walsh had said, when she delivered the cheese.

"But there's two shillings change," Janie pointed out. "The cheese only cost sixpence, and I took half a crown."

"Keep it," Mysie Walsh had insisted. "Run off now, Janie, and bang the door behind you."

There were so many ways to dispose of two shillings, that Janie couldn't decide on one of them. Hide it away till my Mam's broke and give her a real surprise. Or just give her a shilling and me a shilling. Or don't say a word to anybody at all, and spend it myself. Gertie waving in the distance solved the problem and gave Janie a small moment of triumph. "I didn't get the doll from Annie Frigg. But, do you know what, Gertie, I got two bob from Mysie Walsh. As sure as death I did. Look at it."

Chapter Two

DAY had ended in the Lane. But it was not yet night. Night didn't come till the lamp in the causeway was lit. The hooter from the tweed mill had sounded twenty minutes ago; like the belated echo of its dying wail, the mill workers began to clatter up the Lane. This was one of the regular periods in the Lane's existence when Poll, and Battleaxe, and even the Duchess herself, were dispossessed. They ruled their contemporaries, old and bound to the Lane like themselves; they awed the children whose youngness bound them to the precincts of the Lane; but the workers, coming through the causeway in little groups, were impervious to the Duchess's dictates. The Lane was their bed, their supper, their tea and bread and dripping in the morning. Their lives began beyond it. In the Rialto with Pearl White on Monday nights, with the charleston at the Lido on Tuesday nights, nearer home with a threepenny poke of chips, and *It Ain't Gonna Rain No More* scratched out for nothing at Joe's chip shop round the corner. Thursdays were zero nights in their lives. The one night that the Lane could hold them, and even then on unflattering terms: the lack of the price to get beyond it.

The Duchess and her coterie diminished on Thursday night, leaning against the causeway with silent disapproval while the Lane's up-and-coming race held the cobbles and, even more galling, held them in an idiom alien to her Grace; flaunting overmuch of that tin jewellery from Woolworth's, that new store, Nothing Over Sixpence, that had just opened in High Street; drunk with the novelty and prodigality of jewellery so cheap; hands on their hips; shimmying their bodies, like new-fangled whores, for the old-fangled ones like Mysie Walsh and Liza Mac-Vean still just kicked their legs and showed their garters; and the daft tunes they shimmied in rhythm with:

> *But yes,*
> *We have no bananas,*
> *We have no bananas today!*

They had no feeling of protocol either. Didn't care tuppence which lavatory they used. When it had been the Duchess's rule for years that Right Laners used the lavatory by the causeway, and Left Laners used the one up beside the rag-store. They simply used the lavatory nearest their moment of need. And the Duchess strongly suspected, that, as in one other ancient time of need, they also went in two by two.

Fortunately the Duchess's peace of mind was disturbed only on Thursdays in particular, and for this short period of time which was neither night nor day but a transition between. Up the causeway they clattered, this little group of Laners, unknown to either Poll, or Battleaxe, or the Duchess.

"That's wee Lil's Betsy. She's shot up some in this past year."

But they didn't know Betsy. Not now. She had outgrown them. She wasn't old enough to be behind with her rent. She wasn't young enough to have the School Board Man searching her out. And so she eluded them.

"You've got home again, young Betsy?"

"Aye."

"They're saying you're all being put on half-time at the mill. Is that right?"

"*You* tell me!"

"Well!" The Duchess felt weary. "Did you ever hear the like of that for cheek?"

"It's this picture-going!" Poll reflected. "It's making them all like that. They'd bite the hand that feeds them."

"I've never put foot in a picture palace in my life," Battleaxe concluded. "And I've no intention of starting now."

Hugh, the lamp-lighter, set night on its course with one flick from his long pole, and Melodeon Mike set the final seal on it, the clop of his wooden leg distorting the sound of all other passing footsteps. The women round the causeway relaxed. They had come into their own again.

"It's *The Home Fire's Burning* and *The Long Long Trail Awinding* for them tonight, Cocks!" Mike

17

shouted his greeting, knowing that the Duchess had no objection to the rest of the world being cheated as long as she was "in the know".

"I'll just squeeze them out of the old box, give my gammy leg a jerk behind me. And before you can spit, the coppers will be landing on my bonnet. 'Poor Bugger' the folk will be thinking as they eye my leg. 'Poor Sod that's what the war did.' Not, mind you, that *I* ever blamed the war for the loss of my leg. I wouldn't have the lie of it on my soul. But if I were to tell them the truth now, Poll. If I were to turn right round and say I lost my leg in a brawl at Aikey Fair. What do you think they'd say? They'd say, 'Drunken Brute. Serves him right.' That's what they'd say. Folk's minds work queer. Dead queer. If they think I lost it in the war, they're glad because I lost it in a good cause. Or sorry because I lost it in a bad one. All according to how they feel about war. Either way they fling the coppers. What they don't see is that the loss of your leg is the loss of your leg. And it doesn't matter a damn how you lose it. It's still a loss to you."

"And a gain too, though, Mike," Poll pointed out, but without rancour. "I bet you make more out of that gammy leg of yours and that squeeze box than Dodsie Jenner makes out of his lavender bags. And him went through the Dardanelles and all."

"I'll grant you that," Mike agreed, the love of an argument growing big within him. "That's

18

granted. But what has Dodsie Jenner got to show for being through the Dardanelles? Damn all, Poll. If he'd lost an arm now. Or even a coupla fingers itself, his lavender bags would go like nobody's business."

"But Dodsie Jenner lost his mind," Poll protested. "Or at least what mind he did have. I knew him years before the war, he never did have much in his top storey. But what he had he lost after the Dardanelles."

"But a mind's a different matter altogether, Poll," Mike urged. "Nobody knows if you got much of a mind in the first place. So how to hell can they tell when you've lost it? Outsiders I mean. Now I know a cove. He's brother to Bert Wylie's wife. He went through the lot. Got half his face blown off. He sells oranges down in the Green."

"Oh, I know *him*!" Battleaxe broke in. "He's called Pippins for a by-name."

"The same. Pippins. That's him. Well . . ."

"God knows the poor soul can't help only having half a face, but I can never bring myself to buy his oranges," Battleaxe went on. "His face puts me off. I stick to Ned Wheeler when it comes to buying an orange, and of course that's just at the New Year."

"Maybe that then." Mike was impatient of interruptions. "Now, where was I? Oh aye! This cove told me himself one night in The Hole In The Wall . . ."

"I thought Pippins was Pussyfoot," Poll protested. "He was a great one for the Salvation Army for a while."

"He's not that now then," Mike was patient. "Though I did hear tell that it was the Army that helped to set him up in the Green. But when I saw him, he was in The Hole In The Wall. God, Poll, did you ever see a man with his nose shot away down a pint? You don't want to either. But, as I was saying, he told me himself that he makes more money now than he did when he had got all his face. It's proof folk want for their charity, Poll. Something they can see. No. I'll say till my dying day that Dodsie Jenner would have been better off if he'd lost a hand. My luck was just in, I lost my leg in 1916. If I'd lost it in a brawl at Aikey Fair in 1902, I'd have been a dead duck. That's what I mean by 'luck', Poll."

Luck. It was the invincible argument. Even the Duchess was wordless against it. Mike trailed himself away from the safety and comprehension of his own kind, out into the High Street. Only the sound of his melodeon echoed back to them:

. . . *to the land of my dreams.*

"Where the nightingales are singing." Poll sang in solitary accompaniment.

"There was a lot that didn't come back," Battleaxe ventured.

"And them that did come back, came back

worse than they went off," the Duchess added. Even the Duchess, who knew the truth, unconsciously accepted the lie of Mike Melodeon's wooden leg.

Up the Lane at 285 Janie, too, contemplated the results of her "luck".

"Mysie Walsh must be doing all right to give you two bob all in a once," her Mother said, through the hairpins in her teeth. "Did you see my side combs anywhere, Janie? Was Mysie Walsh getting ready to go out, did you notice?"

"I don't know." Janie was absorbed in clearing the table to find room for her book. "She hadn't got her curlers in. She was just lying on top of her bed. She looked fed up. There's a new word for meadow, Mam. A Red Indian word. Muskoday. On the muskoday. The meadow. Muskoday. Musk-o-day. It's in this book. It sounds right fine, doesn't it?"

"Was that what you bought with your two bob?" Liza sounded amused.

"And your tobacco!" Janie protested against this forgetfulness. "You are glad about the tobacco, aren't you, Mam?"

"Yes, of course I am. Get a lace out of one of my other shoes, Janie, this damned lace has snapped!"

"You'd hardly any tobacco left, had you, Mam?"

"No, hardly any. Not out of that shoe, Janie! Use your eyes, that's a brown one."

"Your black shoe must be under the bed then. If you'd had one wish, it would have been for tobacco, wouldn't it?"

"Yes, Janie." Liza's voice came slow and quiet and clear. "I'm glad you bought tobacco. I had hardly any left. And if I'd had one wish, it would have been for tobacco. Now. Have you found my shoe?"

The surprise of Mysie Walsh's two bob was over. Dimly Janie realised that her Mother's gladness at getting, just didn't equal her own gladness in giving.

"Is this the right shoe, Mam?"

"That's it. That's the one." Liza sat absorbed unlacing it. Janie, watching her down-bent head, thought, It's strange, I can hug Mysie Walsh. And smell her hair and I can't do that to my own Mam. Though she's much bonnier than Mysie Walsh. If Janie had been suddenly stricken with blindness she would have had a perpetual picture of her Mother in her memory. Not a photograph. Her Mother had so many faces. But a hundred little images. Each of which was some part of her Mother. And her Mother some part of each. The way her red hair glistened and crept up into little curls when it rained. Her long legs sprawled across the fender. Her tall, swift stride. And her eyes that looked as if they were smiling when the rest of her face was in a rage.

"I'll maybe get diphtheria like Gertie did," Janie thought, watching her, "and have to go away in the ambulance. Maybe my Mam will hug me like Mysie Walsh does, then."

"The Salacs are here, Janie," Gertie shouted from the lobby below. "There's going to be testimony and saving. Hurry up, or you'll miss it all."

"Well." Liza's eyes were smiling. "That's something, Janie. Aren't you going?"

"I was going." Janie was undecided. "But there's a penny for the gas now. And I've got my book. The only thing is the Salacs only come on Saturdays. If I don't go tonight, I'll miss it all for a week."

"And you want both things at once, Janie?" Liza was quizzical. "Well. Nothing like it if you can get it. I'm away now. If you're in your bed before I get back, see and leave the sneck off the door." Liza, remembering something, popped her head round the door again: "Take my tip, Janie. If you go to the Salacs tonight, you'll still have your book left for tomorrow. That way of it, you'll get both things. But not at once, that's what makes it tough. Don't forget. Leave the sneck off the door for me."

Five minutes later Janie and Gertie were pushing their way through the crowd gathered round the street lamp.

"You've made us late," Gertie grumbled. "And you've got an awful smell."

"I know." Janie was unoffended. "It's cats.

I'd to crawl under our bed. And Mysie Walsh's cat always comes in and does it under our bed. O look, Gertie, Annie Frigg's got a good shot in. I bet you anything she'll cry tonight, and give testimony, and kiss the Salacs. I love it when she does that. She's so funny."

The crowd gathered round the Salvation Army was unchanging. The old Laners, who preferred the light of the lamp and the company to the darkness and loneliness of their rooms. The deformed Laners. White, fanatical, and selfish, not only laying claim to the best position round the lamp, but forcing a prior claim on God Himself, whining their Hallelujahs right up to the top of the lamp, where they thought the Mercy Seat must lie. And of course always the children of the Lane who loved a noise anyhow. Later the drunks, reluctant to go home, would join the group. And if testimony wasn't over by the time they arrived, their testimony would be the most fervent of the lot. Beyond the group, leaning against the causeway, were the objective spectators, the Duchess, Poll, and Battleaxe. Without need of salvation in their own opinions, they nevertheless enjoyed the antics of their neighbours who were so very obviously in need of it.

> *He's the lily of the valley.*
> *He's the bright and morning star.*

Despite themselves, the objective spectators hummed the chorus. It was familiar. Like saying God bless you. Or God curse you. Something you had always said.

> *He's the fairest of ten thousand*
> *To my soul.*
> *To my soul.*

But Janie knew that she would always remember the sudden green and silver image the words had brought to the Lane at dusk. Gertie, unmoved by words and images, was becoming irritable.

"I thought they were going to be saving us tonight. It's a damned shame if they don't. So it is."

"Wheesht," admonished Chae Tastard, normally one of the best cursers in the Lane, but momentarily under the spell of the Salvationists. "It's terrible the language that's on you two bairns. And the napkins hardly off your arses yet."

And even more terrible the crowd's sudden and complete desertion of the Salvationists. It was Betsy's young Alan, who started the whisper:

"Mysie Walsh's done herself in. Hanged herself. The bobbies are up at 284 now."

"Making a right barney about her being cut down before they got the chance to do it themselves," Betsy added to the information.

"Who cut her down, Son?" Battleaxe demanded

like a furious general who had been overlooked, but still had a right to know. "Who was it that cut her down?"

"Chae did. Chae Tastard, with his sharp cobbler's knife."

"Liars!" Janie screamed in a small panic. "She isn't dead. I took cheese to her."

"Yeah?" Betsy's young Alan shot his tongue out at Janie and passed on, anxious to spread all the news to the more important grown-ups. "And do you know what? A bit of cheese was stuck in her mouth when they took the rope off."

Ted Howe, only drunkenly comprehending the news, forced his way through the crowd. "Take my boots off when I die. When I die." And beneath the lamp the Salvationists sang for their own edification:

> *Dare to do right.*
> *Dare to be true.*
> *God who created you*
> *Cares for you, too.*

For the crowd had deserted them and were following Ted towards the door of Mysie Walsh who was.

"Them," Poll was saying, watching the police-guarded door morosely. "Them that takes their own lives, don't get to rest in consecrated ground. It's yon bit of common ground behind the gaswork for them."

"I saw this coming," Battleaxe added, with

the pride of a prophet whose vision has come true. " 'Mark my words,' I said to my man just the night before last, 'Mysie Walsh will come to a bad end. She'll never die in her bed.' "

"Not with the life she led," the Duchess agreed. "Running around with every Tom, Dick, and Harry. Enough to drive you mad, through time. And that time she was in hospital with the poomonia. I know what she had. And it wasn't poomonia either. I cut my wisdom teeth too early to be mistaken."

The next of kin pushed her way through the crowd. Battleaxe, furious at her prerogative in getting past the Bobby unchallenged, spat out her commentary:

"See her? No show without Punch. Last time she saw Mysie Walsh she was pulling the hair out of her. Said she wouldn't spit in Mysie Walsh's direction because she owed her ten bob."

A sense of fear took hold of Chae Tastard's small wife. Fear of what lay beyond the police-guarded door, fear of Battleaxe's anger, fear of everything. "Death pays all debts," she said in a quiet and already defeated attempt to escape.

The Duchess began to laugh harshly. "That way of it, Lil, the sooner we're all in our wee, black boxes the better."

The next of kin was coming out. "Is she dead?" shouted Battleaxe, waiving aside personal differences out of a zeal for truth.

"Stone dead." The next of kin was glad of a

truce which lent her an attentive ear. "As dead as a door nail. You wouldn't know her. You wouldn't know a bit of her. Her face black. Her tongue swollen twice the size of your fist. And a lump of cheese fit to choke her on its own stuck in her gullet."

"I took the cheese to her," Janie shouted from amongst the women's shawls. "But I didn't know. Honest to God I didn't."

The shawls wheeled round in attack.

"You shouldn't know either," Battleaxe shouted, jealously eyeing the small girl who had last seen the corpse alive. "You're too young to give evidence, anyhow."

"You should have been in your bed long ago," the Duchess added. "If you were mine! But, thank God you're no' mine. Standing there all eyes and ears. Beat it now. Before I take the lights from you!"

The policeman saved Janie from sudden extinction. "The show's over for tonight," he said, with just the amount of humour needed for the crowd's mood. "You lot got no homes to go to?"

"Only just," cried Battleaxe, speaking for them all. "The rent's behind."

The crowd had gone, taking with them the cover which they had flung over the tenement. Mysie Walsh's window, covered with a blanket, lay exposed to Janie and Gertie. Gertie who lived two doors away flaunted her own safety: "I'd just hate to be you, Janie, having to pass Mysie Walsh's door tonight. Maybe she'll jump out on you."

"She can't. She's dead." Janie used reason to fight fancy, but didn't succeed. "Come on up with me, Gertie. Just till my Mam comes home."

"I can't, I've got to go home or else I'll get a belting. But she can't touch you, Janie," and as if regretting her reassurances, Gertie shouted over her shoulder as she disappeared: "I wouldn't be you for anything, Janie. She might just jump out on you."

All black and her tongue purple, Janie thought, as the wooden stairs creaked beneath her feet. Ready to jump out on me when I reach second landing. For death, and this was Janie's first, near experience of it, could suddenly translate the loved and the living into the ghostly and the frightening. The scream poised itself in Janie's throat, ready for its flight through the tenement, the moment Mysie Walsh jumped out of death, through the door. And not really ready when the moment came. Only the figure who leapt from beside her door, heard the cry that was a substitute for the scream.

"Shut your mouth, you little bastard. Do you want the whole house woken up?"

The dead don't speak so. The livingness of the words calmed Janie into surveying the speaker. It was a man. Her Mother suddenly appeared

from behind him, annoyance in her voice.
"Leave the bairn alone."

"Yours?" the man asked.

"Aye. My first mistake. And my last one."

The man jingled coppers in his pocket. "Like
to go and get yourself some chips, hen?"

"I can't. Chip shop's shut," Janie said, contemplating him gratefully, since, whoever he was,
he just wasn't Mysie Walsh back from the dead.

"Find out the time for us, then."

"It's gone eleven. Gertie and me heard the
clock not long since."

"Scram then." The man was growing angry.
"Make yourself scarce for God's sake."

"She's my bairn," Liza said resentfully, coming
towards Janie. "Look, luv, run into Mysie
Walsh's for some coppers for the gas. Here's
sixpence. Move over, you. Till the bairn gets
past."

"I can't," Janie stood impassively. "Mysie
Walsh's dead."

"Don't be daft. Don't act it," Liza said harshly
in the darkness. "I spoke to Mysie Walsh when I
went out."

"She's dead since." Janie stood small and im-
pregnable in the safety of truth. "She hanged
herself. The bobbies were here and all. Chae
Tastard cut her down with his big knife."

Liza stared at Mysie Walsh's door, and backed
away from it, no longer aware of the man:
"Come on, Janie. It's high time you and me

were in our bed. Mind your feet on the first step. It won't be there much longer."

"What about me?" The man's voice came plaintively behind them.

"You can keep," Liza called down, as if she had forgotten him.

"What about my dough? I paid you, didn't I?"

"And I should have got you between the eyes with your lousy dough." There was anger in Liza's voice. But Janie sensed that this anger wasn't directed at her. It was as if herself and her Mother were in league, against the man. "Mind your feet now, bairn," her Mother said. Warmly, intimately. The two of them taking care of each other on the stairs.

"You damned two-timer. You prick tormentor." The man's voice came furiously from below. "I paid you, didn't I?"

"And here's your money." The sudden clatter of coppers in the darkness, the anger in Liza's voice, frightened the man. He mumbled himself down, and out of hearing.

"You stay here, Mam," Janie cried, when he had gone. "Just wait for me here, and I'll look for the money you threw. It's on the landing somewhere."

Liza waited without protest. Throwing the money had been a sincere gesture, but a reckless one. "There was two bob. A two-bob bit, and sixpence of coppers," she shouted to Janie. "Can you see, or will I light the lobby gas?"

"I've found the two-bob bit," Janie answered. "Maybe the pennies have rolled under Mysie Walsh's door!"

But Mysie Walsh was dead. At the other side of the door. Her face all black and her tongue all purple. Janie had forgotten. Now she remembered, and ran upstairs without the pennies, to where her Mother waited.

Chapter Three

THE Lane came reluctantly to life. Its occupants, unwilling to face the first shock of early morning coldness, were even more unwilling to miss a moment of Mysie Walsh's funeral.

No one was sure of the exact time of this event. "Before dinner-time," Battleaxe said, tilting her tea-leaves into the dustbin. "Before the sun rises full."

"Myself now," maintained Poll, waiting in the bin queue, "had the idea that suicides were buried after the sun goes down. I know that the sun hasn't got to shine on them. But one can never be sure about that."

"I know one thing," the Duchess concluded, "if Pinner has the undertaking, and he usually has the Poor Law burials, he'll want it over and done with by the time The Hole In The Wall opens."

Nothing was sure at this grey time of the morning, except that the burial of Mysie Walsh would be a sly, dark thing. As hurried and as secret as her death had been. The women round the dustbin felt that she had cheated them by dying without first informing them. But, by Christ, they weren't going to be done out of her funeral too.

"Not if I stand holding up this wall till

midnight," vowed Battleaxe, planting her teapot firmly between her feet, settling her back comfortably against the causeway and casting a resentful glance over the other women, arriving to stake for themselves a place with a view.

Wee Lil, flopping down the cobbles in her man's shoes, felt Battleaxe's resentment rush towards her and directed it away from herself with panting haste:

"You lot hear the shindy, last night? That Liza MacVean and one of her pick-ups. You wouldn't have thought there was a corpse in the tenement. Chewing the fat like hell they were. Sounded like they were both up against Mysie Walsh's door. No shame in the world. Some folk haven't. And Mysie Walsh stone dead on the other side of the door."

Poll felt suddenly ribald. "Well. What's the odds? Mysie Walsh couldn't take it herself anymore anyhow." Poll's laugh rose solitary and, shamed by its own loneliness, darted thinly into silence.

"There is," admonished the Duchess, "a time and a place for allusions to other folks' weakness. And Mysie Walsh is dead."

"And me thinking Mysie Walsh came alive, last night," Janie confided to Gertie, on the way down to join the watchers. "As sure as God. I thought it was her when the man jumped out on me."

"What man?" Gertie asked, with the sleep still over her.

"Just some man," Janie answered swiftly. "After Mysie Walsh likely." For it was known that men went for Mysie Walsh. And Janie hoped it wasn't known that men went for her Mother, too.

"And her dead," Gertie said, completely side-tracked. "No wonder my Mam says men are just beasts."

Battleaxe was right. Before the sun rose full, two horses, pulling the hearse, drew up in front of the tenement.

"Only two horses." Janie was disappointed. "Balaclava had four, with black feathers over their heads when she was buried."

"That's because this is no' a real funeral," young Alan shouted, knowing everything, loudly.

"No. But the corpse is real enough, Son," Chae Tastard answered. And he should know, Janie thought, watching him curiously, for he had cut down the corpse. He had seen somebody dead. She stared at his face to find the imprint so strange a seeing must have left upon it. His face looked the same as it always did in his dark, cobbler's shop, his eyes pale and peering, with yellow stuff stuck in the corners. And when Chae spoke again, there was no more wonder to him.

"I could hardly get near her to cut her down.

35

She hadn't opened her window for weeks, surely. Her room stank to Heaven."

As the undertaker's men shouldered the coffin, past condemnation turned to present pity.

"She wasna' the worst." Battleaxe dabbed tearless eyes. "If she'd got a bob she'd break it, and let you have the tanner."

"And that time my Ned was knocked off the mill, she never saw him without a Woodbine," Poll said, edging Gertie off the kerb, to get a better look at the coffin. "What a sin. Not even a flower allowed on it."

Battleaxe assented sadly. "A funeral's no' a funeral without a flower."

"What you never had you never miss," Janie's Mother broke in, appearing so suddenly behind the coffin, that she scattered the crowd. "And, what's more, Mysie Walsh's in the best place." She didn't give the surprised women time to sharpen their tongues for the defence of such callousness to a corpse, but strode through them. Not even having the decency to stand still in that moment when Pinner crowned himself with his long, funeral hat and lifted his black cane to motion the hearse forward.

"Well," said the Duchess when she had got her breath back. "Of all the hard-hearted bitches, that Liza MacVean takes the cake."

"She'll miss Mysie Walsh for one," Poll prophesied. "She always knew where to go for the price of a bag of cinders. And that young

Janie of hers always knew where to go for a bite."

"What's more," Battleaxe said, looking furtively round to see where young Janie was, "what's more, you'd expect Liza to cut up rough. Her and Mysie Walsh being partners in the business, as you might say. When one has too many clients, she handed the other the overflow."

Janie had at last caught up with her Mother. Furiously. Accusingly. "You didn't cry once, Mam. Everybody was sorry for Mysie Walsh, and cried, except you."

"There's nothing to cry for." Liza didn't look at the child. And didn't slacken her stride. "Nothing at all. Death's the poor man's best friend. Burns said that. And do you know something? He was quite right. I'll be back a bit earlier tonight. Here's tuppence for you. And I've left coppers for the gas."

"How much?" Gertie demanded, closing in.

"Tuppence."

"But she said she left coppers for the gas, Janie."

"So she did."

"Well, you won't be needing the gas for ages. We can have the lot between us. Birnie's have got gingerbread men. Great fat ones. They only cost two a penny."

The Lane settled down into an apathy edged with restiveness. Mysie Walsh's funeral had ended too soon, leaving the rest of the day to stretch interminably before the women, leaning against the causeway, with their arms folded across their bosoms.

Janie and Gertie were not caught up in the surrounding apathy. The Lane was the world. And, being so, ever willing to offer up some new distraction. Like the Duchess's scillas in the window-box. A blaze of blue.

"It's bound to be summer soon," Janie said, spying them. "The Duchess's scillas are out, now. And then it'll be Waifs and Strays' picnic. I'm going to eat till I burst, this year. I was too excited to eat last year. And I wished for days after that I'd eaten everything."

"Me too," Gertie agreed. "I'm going to get tore into all the stuff this time. Only it'll be a long time till it comes."

"And I'll have new boots, soon," Janie went on, trying to reach the picnic sooner, by marking time off with small landmarks. "I'm due for a ticket for new boots soon."

"My Mam won't apply for a ticket any more." Gertie was rueful. "Because the man that gives you the tickets tried to put his hand up her clothes. My Dad wasn't half flaming. Said he would knock him into next week. But Mam said not to. He gives the tickets for Free Coal too, you see. And he mightn't have given us one. Not if my Dad had bashed him one."

An old envy of Gertie's Dad crept over Janie. That big coal carter, with a voice that could frighten Cruelty Inspectors and Sanitary Men, making them small and wordless and quick to disappear. Gertie didn't know what it was to sneck the door and hide under the bed when they came. Her Dad was there to attack the attacker, shouting right down the Lane after him:

"She'll go to school when she's got boots to her feet. And that'll be when I can afford them."

Not like us, Janie thought. My Mam is afraid of them all. And I get frightened for her. And there's nobody to knock the Free Boot Man into next week if he tries to put his hand up our clothes.

Janie had created a Father for herself. It was easier to make a completely new Father, than to build from the scant facts she knew about the original:

"You've got your Father's eyes," her Mother would say when she was in a temper. "Real wicked eyes. And he was a bad one. By God he was."

Or, when her Mother was in a mood, mellowed sometimes by the Lane's own mood, warm and kind, gathering its occupants round its causeway in an expansive oneness, with Poll's voice singing over them:

Abie, Abie, Abie my boy
What are you waiting for now?
You promised to marry me
One day in June.
It's never too late,
But it's never too soon.

39

Janie's Mother would squeeze Janie's hand, whispering through Poll's song: "Your Father could take music out of a tin whistle. That he could. He had so much music to him."

It had been difficult to take these solitary, contradictory facts and build one complete Father out of them. So Janie, perforce, had given life to a new Father. And death too. Death eliminated awkward questions to which Janie hadn't got the answer. Gertie had accepted it all as if it wasn't a lie at all:

"So that's why you and your Mam go up to the Cemetery every Sunday?"

"Don't be daft!" Janie had protested, momentarily forgetting her fabrication. "My Mam just goes for the walk, and I go to pinch the flowers out of the green bins. Yon little white angel we have on our mantelpiece, I took that too, once. We do look at my Father's grave," she added hurriedly, remembering. "Do you know what it says on his stone, Gertie? It says *Asleep In Jesus*. You can come with me one Sunday to see for yourself."

Dusk had drawn the Lane into its folds. The women at the causeway had become part of its pattern, absorbed into the greyness of the walls they leant against. Battleaxe leapt in sudden protest against this loss of her individuality. "It's gone six," she said, bending to retrieve her teapot between her feet. "My Joe's due home."

"What's more," the Duchess cried, coming to life and darting for second place at the pump, "this perisher of a pump's froze, or choked up or something. We'll be all night squeezing a drop of water out of it."

"Not me!" Battleaxe defended her nickname. "Not if I've got to rattle the guts out of the damned thing. My Joe works for his supper, so he does. Not like some I could name."

Poll rose glinting-eyed to the bait: "My Hughie would work too, if he'd got work. But he was never the one to lick the Town Council's arse. If he'd licked a bit more, he might have still been on the dust-cart."

"Meaning what?" Battleaxe's ears flew back and flicked. "If you're insinuating that my Joe's a Yes Man."

"I'm insinuating nothing." Poll was beyond fear. " I'm saying straight out that your Joe wasn't knocked off with the rest of them, because his wife's tongue's handy for the Council's ears. Who was it that nipped up to the Town Hall and reported wee Lil's bugs to the Sanitary? Tell us that!"

Wee Lil, proud of being the sudden centre of interest, gasped pink-faced and pleadingly: "I don't know who reported my bugs. I only know that I've lived in the Lane all my days, and I've never reported nobody. You all know that."

"Because you haven't got the guts. That's why!" Battleaxe's skirt wheeled round wee Lil.

"None of you have got any guts. Except when the beer's inside you!"

"There's going to be a fight," Gertie prodded Janie excitedly. "Poll and Battleaxe are getting tore into each other at the pump. Come on and watch. Come on, Janie. Don't be such a fearty."

Janie was a fearty. Feared of so many things that left Gertie unafraid. Like the women when they fought. Not looking like women any more. But dark and furious and whirling like witches Janie had seen in story books. Janie's fear was never for the actual, but for the imagined. It could have been her Mother, lying there mauled and vulgar with her clothes up round her head, and blood trickling from her mouth. But that will never happen, Janie vowed to herself. Because I would fight for my Mam. I'd be so frightened for her, that I wouldn't have fear left for myself at all. I'd become as strong as anything. I know I would. I'd batter the women's heads against the cobbles, and squeeze their faces, and trample all over them with my feet. I'd just kill them, if they ever touched my Mam.

"Here's Sam's Ernie coming to throw sawdust on the blood," Gertie said with regretful finality, as if this ritual truly ended the fight. "Anyhow, Battleaxe won, Poll had to get stitches."

"Ten stitches," young Alan assured them in the passing. "My mother went with her in the ambulance to Casualty. Said she didn't half bleed."

"Come on, Janie," Gertie urged. "The sawdust's on the blood now, there's nothing more to see."

But there was. Through the sawdust Janie still saw the blood, a small, dark loch submerged between cobbles that had become mountains.

"Come on. Down to the Green to see Beulah."

"Don't you two be going and bringing lice back from that lousy tinker," warned the Duchess, overhearing the suggestion. "We've got enough troubles without getting some of her lice into the bargain."

"Anyhow," wee Lil contributed, "you won't find Beulah down on the Green, she's doing time."

"Wee Lil's a liar," Janie hissed, as they ran towards the Green. "Beulah's out. I saw her in the street cadging rabbit skins."

Chapter Four

THE Green was as much part of the Lane as the communal pump in the causeway. If you weren't in the Lane you were "down at the Green". There was no third alternative. Even if there had been, you would have been out of your mind to have chosen it in preference to the Green.

The summer through, the Green's chair-o-planes, whirling high, blistered with colour and blared with music. The Devil's Own Din was how the sedate residents of Hill Terrace described it in a protest to the Lord Provost and Town Council, but to the Laners who were the true lovers of the Green it was music.

It was *If you were the only Girl in the World* sung in a frenzied, birling chorus by the angels and cherubs painted on the awnings of the chair-o-planes; it was the voices of spielers imploring, hectoring you into seeing The Strongest Man in The World, as crowned heads of Europe were privileged to see him, and You that wasn't a crowned head of any place at all, what in the Name were you standing waiting for, when you could walk right in. A tanner a time. And the best tanner's worth you'd ever be likely to see this side of heaven, that is if you were ever likely to get there at all.

It was thin men at coconut stalls wheedling you into three balls for tuppence, and a prize every time.

It was the show's women in bright head-scarves shouting to each other from the steps of their caravans about their washing and their children; of how liver had been ninepence at Auchnasheen last week, but would be less by the time they got to Auchnashelach. Auchnasheen and Auchnashelach, Udale Bay and Duirinish. The bright, far-sounding names of places drifting up through streamers and balloons as bright and remote as themselves.

It was the sound of a smack on a child's bare bottom and a rising scream of protest.

It was all noise gathered into the chair-o-planes in the centre, held there, and flung over and outwards in a singing crescendo of adoration:

> *O, O, how I love you,*
> *How I love you,*
> *My dearest Swanee.*

The Green had its own social scale. Lord John Sanger's circus was the cream of its aristocracy. When the circus arrived, the chair-o-planes, the Strong Man, the coconut stalls, withdrew from the centre of the Green and huddled themselves away in a more remote direction, like younger sons knowing their proper place but still dependent.

45

When winter came and the last circus elephant had trumpeted its way to the station, and the show's last caravan rumbled along the North Road, leaving only faded, brown circles on the Green's grass to prove that they had ever been there at all, the tinkers, the third and last grade of the Green's society, took over.

The show they put on was less spectacular than that of their forerunners. Their caravans were still horse-drawn, shaped like wagons and made of green canvas. Their tents were small and brown. But the tinkers also had the magical facility of rolling far-sounding places round their tongues.

Aikey Fair, "Where the ale cost only tuppence and a tanner bocht a gill." Raffan Market, its horse sales with brown, furtive tinkers "wheezing gajes for jowldie"—taking country men for suckers. Blairgowrie, the great trek southwards to the berry picking, and "I'll show ye the road and the miles to Dundee, Janie." Still southwards but nearer home, to the farming lands up Donside way, "There's no place like Aberdeenshire, Janie, and no folk so fine as them that bide by Don."

And, though Janie had never been beyond the Lane, through her own imagination and through close companionship with Beulah, the Green's oldest tinker, she knew their ways and their meeting places almost as well as she knew the Lane.

Janie's ambition was to be a real tinker some-day. Meanwhile, under Beulah's expert eye, she had learned to "pick rags", cadge rabbit skins, stock the "swag" in Beulah's basket. And given money, Janie could have purchased Beulah's "swag" herself, in correct proportion to its sell-ing powers. Shoe-laces, buttons, reels of cotton, a line that even the harassed, hard-up cottar wives would not close their doors against. Milk bowls and fancy butter dishes for the more opulent farmers' wives, brooches and hair-slides for her brosy servant girl, for the great secret was to get round the servant before you attacked her mis-tress. Bluebirds flying from long sticks for the lawful bairns of both cottar and farm wife, and the unlawful bairns of the servants. It was a fact, garnered from Beulah, that even when money was scarce, it was never so scarce but it would be taken out from the hoard, hidden in some antrin jug, to quieten the roar the bairns set up, when they caught their first glimpse of a bluebird flying from a stick.

One of the intensely happy moments in Janie's life was a moment like this, when she saw Beulah's caravan rising high out of the dusk, with the fire burning redly outside it, and Beulah herself coory-ing over it, stirring her pot.

"I told you Beulah was out of the nick, Gertie. She's making rice. I can get the smell of it."

Janie suddenly realised that she was very

hungry. "We'll get some if Beulah's had a good day gathering rags. She'll be in a right good humour."

Beulah *was* in a good humour. Her release from jail lay largely and benignly over her, smiling in the brown creases of her face, dancing defiance in the jingle of her long, brass earrings. She greeted Janie and Gertie exuberantly:

"God bless us. Over the bones of my poor Mother that's dead, I thought you'd gone clean off the face of the earth, Janie. Gospel truth I did. Did you forget your road to the caravan? Or, was it maybe that you found a better friend than old Beulah?"

A protest against such treachery rose to Janie's lips to be stifled by the smell rising overwhelmingly near and sweet from the pot.

"No, Beulah," Janie struggled for an explanation that wouldn't offend Beulah too deeply. "We didn't come because we heard you was away for a while."

"A while!" Beulah protested, scandalised by such understatement. "Fourteen days without the option of a fine. That's what I was away for. Fourteen days. And me with no more than a wee hauf and a brown inside me. Not another drop passed my lips. And there's the God's truth for you. There, sit you down on the rabbit skins, and I'll tell you dead straight—between you and me and the mare—without a word of a lie, what's behind me and the fourteen days."

Beulah's spoon stopped stirring, she thrust her face nearer the fire, and Janie held back her breath for the momentousness of a secret.

"They lift me to spring-clean their jails for them," Beulah whispered, her whisper cracking with the injustice of it all. "I can be as drunk's a Lord in November, or even in February for that matter of it, and the Bobbies turn a blind eye to me, but, this is the Gospel truth, the moment the first ray of spring sun blinks through and shows up all the dirt in Barclamp Jail, every Bobby in the force is on the look-out for me. Folk can be robbed in their sleep. Or murdered in their beds. Does the Bobbies care? No! They're too busy looking for me. They know it will be a feather in their bonnet for lifting me. For there's none that scrubs out their jail as thorough as I do. Free gratis and for nothing. But it's the last time they'll lift me in the spring. I vow that to my Maker. The flat-footed bucks!"

Beulah's spoon went whirling into action again: the renewed thick smell of rice rising into the air keened Janie's hunger into a pain. The solution to Beulah's problem suddenly seemed so much simpler than the solution to her own hunger.

"But you could go away in the spring, Beulah. Miles away in your caravan. They couldn't catch you to spring-clean the jail then."

The solution didn't appeal to Beulah. "My

reputation," she said in an offended voice, "my reputation as a scrubber has gone before me. South to the Border country. And as far north as John o' Groats itself. I've spring-cleaned all their jails for them in my time. But this is the last time. The very last time."

"I'm glad you're never going back to the nick, Beulah." Janie was anxious to atone for offending Beulah, and even more anxious to taste the rice. "Honest I am. You're always so good when you're making your rice."

Beulah stared intently at her pot as if all prophecy lay inside it, then lifted her head sharply up from the pot and fixed Janie with her bright eyes:

"You're byordinar fond of rice, aren't you, Bronian?" Janie, trapped by the glint of Beulah's eyes and the bright gleam of her earrings, said, staring:

"I do love your rice, Beulah. It's the best and sweetest and hottest rice in the world."

"I know you love it. Bless you," Beulah answered, smiling contentedly into her pot. "And because I know that, something happened to me the day. I was just turning into Birnie's for my half ounce of black twist, when a thought took hold of me there where I stood, on Birnie's doorstep. And a voice said to me, Beulah, you can't have your half of twist this night: You just can't have it. Do you know something? Janie is coming to see you tonight. And she's the bairn after your own heart. And you know how fond she is of a tattie of rice. If you buy your twist you won't have a brown farthing left to buy rice. And Janie won't get the fine taste of it on her tongue this night. So I bought the rice and went without my roll of twist." Beulah sighed and stirred her pot in silence before she lifted her eyes to Janie. "And do you know something, Janie? God above and my Mother that's dead knows that I didn't begrudge buying the rice for you. But, all day, my tongue's been like a bit of bark in my mouth for want of a smoke. And it's a queer dwamie feeling I've got in my head. As if I'm going to fall down on my face any minute. And not rise again. I wouldn't be sorry to be not rising again with the dwam that's come over me. I'd be glad. For peace to my bones."

"Would a smoke take the dwam away from you, Beulah?" Janie asked in a panic.

Beulah considered this: "It might just help. Might just take the edge of the dwam away from me, like. Give me my second wind back to fight against the terrible things that's killing me. But where in the world is even a pipeful to be had?"

"I'll beg some tobacco for you, Beulah. My Mam's got some. But she's out. But I'll beg some for you." Janie sprang to her feet. "I'll beg it from the first man I see. I just won't come back till I've got a pipeful for you."

Beulah looked swiftly up from her pot as if anticipation had already lessened her dwam.

51

"Say it's for your Grandmother, Janie, Bron-ian. Her that's just at death's door. Say it's the last thing she'll need from Man. Or from God either, for that of it."

Janie flew across the Green, spurred on by Beulah's promises: "Your rice will be done to a T by the time you get back, dearie. And I'll leave a McPhee's mark on this little friend of yours, if she knocks back one bit of rice that was meant for you."

Begging, in Janie's eyes, was the one distasteful aspect in the tinker's otherwise perfect way of life. There was no adventure to it, and the only ability it needed was the instinct to pick out the "right" face. Janie had never to beg for her own needs. There were better ways of satisfying them. The surest way to get a penny was to scour the football grounds for empty beer bottles and sell them back to the beer shops at half rate. A fair bargain, since the bottles hadn't belonged to you in the first place. More remunerating, but less infallible, was to stand outside The Hole In The Wall on Saturday night, bump into the first drunk man you saw, weep loudly, pretending he had bumped into you. That was usually a sure three-pence forced into your palm. Sometimes it was sixpence if the man was drunk enough. For her other needs, Janie confined herself to the dustbins in High Street. The paper she scribbled on came from the bin of MacFarlane, Stationer and Book-seller. Her fruit, usually well out of season, from the Greengrocer's bin. Her dolls came from further afield, from the City dump. Being completely unselfish, Janie dragged home most of the bits that furnished her Mother's room from the dump, too. Gertie was truly the sleeping partner, in this business of existing; she shared the profits, while Janie put in most of the capital required. Discrimination, and being on the spot at the right time. Standing here, watching for the "right" face to come up, had none of the excitement of discovering a new shop and its new, unexplored dustbin.

Meanwhile Gertie was curiously watching the renewed energy with which Beulah stirred her pot.

"You're feeling a bit better now, Beulah?"

"A thochtie better maybe, bairn. A thochtie," Beulah agreed with some reluctance. "The thocht of getting a bit of tobacco. Mark you, that's nearly as good as the tobacco itself lying tight in the bowl of my pipe, and myself drawing away fine and regular, with the good rich spit to it. Now, this is what the thocht does." Beulah relaxed, talking slowly and comfortably in rhythm with her stirring. "My old Father could break in a colt with the best of them; the Williamsons, the Robertsons, aye, and the Stewarts. Now, when he was lying at death's door at Raffan Market that was. A wild market that. Such as you won't see again. At least one of our breed getting killed at it, and a dozen getting broken heads and needing

the hospital or women's care in the tents. That is
if we weren't needing care ourselves. For we
fought each other too, you see. God above we did.
Nothing personal in it. Nothing at all. Each just
for the sake of sticking up for her own man. At
the end of the night we were so muddled up that
we fought both friend and foe alike. And no
offence taken when it was all over. None. We'd
bid each other God speed. Tell each other of the
best farms for a 'touch' on the road. Roll away
in our wagons and forget everything till a year
passed and Raffan Market came around again.
Then we'd suddenly remember what this cove had
called us last year, or the names this manashe had
spat at us the year before. And, God bless you,
before we knew what had happened, we were in
the middle of another fight. But it was all just
part of Raffan Market, the fights were. And the
thing you've got for Raffan Market now is a poor
thing at its best. No murders. No broken heads.
Not a Man Jack in it that does more than commit
a breach of peace. A poor thing compared to the
Raffan Market I knew."

"But what about your old Father, Beulah?
Him that started the story? Him that was lying at
death's door?" Gertie asked, eager for Beulah to
go on with her story.

"Oh, him is it?" Beulah was not to be dis-
tracted from her vision of bygone Raffan Markets.
"He died in his bed, that's all. The only McPhee
for ninety years to disgrace us by dying in his bed.

That was at Raffan Market too." Beulah stared into her pot again as if seeing within it all the Raffan Markets she had ever known. "Mind you, he was a smart man, my father. None his marrow when it came to making an old mare look as young and lifey as a two-year-old, tarring its grey hairs, till the rains came or the heat of the sun came and the tar melted leaving the grey hairs and the bald patches for even the blind to see. But of course he'd sold the horse by that time, so it was imagination that made us laugh when the sun came, at the thought of the gaje who had bought the horse. Oh, and he could blow a thin horse up too. Simple enough to do that. But you've got to sell the horse quick. Before it does its natural function, and blows out all you've stuffed its behind with. But that's another tale."

"I've got tobacco for you, Beulah," Janie shouted from the distance. "I told you I'd get some for you. Look, there's more than a pipeful here."

Beulah sniffed the tobacco suspiciously, "Scented dirt. Too fine altogether," she said, rubbing it between her fingers. "It hasn't got the body in it to lie dour and dark in my pipe. This dirt will blaze up like shavings."

"A gentleman gave it to me," Janie protested, "with a hat on and gloves and everything, a real barrie gaje he was," she emphasised in Beulah's own language, proud of her knowledge of it. "And I had an awful job to get it from him at all. I'd

55

to tell him my name and address and everything."

"And did you?" Beulah looked up sharply. "Your real name?"

"Yes," Janie answered, "I haven't got another name."

"You could have given yourself another name," Beulah grumbled. "Folk that know you don't need to ask your name. And them that don't know you have no right to ask it. Mind on that and you'll walk safe. It wouldn't have been one of 'them', would it?" Beulah asked in a furtive whisper.

Janie cast her mind's eye over "them". "No. No, Beulah, it wasn't one of 'them'. This was a big gentleman. The Cruelty Man's wee with a moustache, I know him. And it wasn't the School Board Man, he's got a uniform. And the Bobbies have got uniforms. It wasn't any of them."

"I'm not so sure." Beulah was unappeased. " 'They' dress up different to catch folk out. Did you tell him it was for your Grandmother?"

"Yes. He asked her name. I gave your name, because my Grandmother doesn't smoke. She just hates pipes. Even my Mam has to hide her pipe in the top of her stocking when we got to see Grandmother. He took it all down in a wee book."

A sudden fury took hold of Beulah. Her wooden spoon clattered into the pot.

"In the name of God. The Sheriff will have me up in front of him for aiding and abetting. Thirty

56

days I'll get this time. Haven't you got a Grand-mother of your own, without taking the McPhee name in vain. I wouldn't spit on the breed of you, bairn. What about your own Grandmother's name for the gaje's book?"

"I couldn't give her name." Janie was fright-ened by the anger in Beulah's voice. "I just couldn't give my Grandmother's name. She doesn't smoke. And she's a lady, you see."

"A *lady* is it?" Beulah's face closed nearer till it almost touched Janie's own face. "So it's Grand-mother is a lady? But the McPhee has to feed it. Highland pride and scab and hunger!" A harsh quality had entered Beulah's voice. "The lady Grandmother doesn't give you rice, does she? No. No fear of that."

Janie's fear left her, she was filled with an in-comprehensible anger against Beulah. "My Grand-mother gives me soup. She gives me it in a blue bowl with roses round it. And a spoon that shines like anything. My face looks twice as fat when I look at it in her shining spoon. When we have pudding we get another clean spoon. She would give me rice too, if I stayed with her. But it's too far away for me to stay with her. I don't know her address, but I know the road to her house. It's away in the country. In Grandmother's country."

"We would have got some rice too," Gertie

57

grumbled, when herself and Janie were safely away from Beulah's curses. "We'd have got it if you hadn't said that your Grandmother's a lady. That made Beulah awful mad. Besides," Gertie went on suspiciously, "it's a funny thing, Janie, I've never once seen your Grandmother. She never comes to the Lane, does she now?"

"No. And do you know why she doesn't come, Gertie, she doesn't like the smell of cats. She lives in a red house on top of a hill. It shines like anything. I'm glad she doesn't come to the Lane to see us. Someday I'll ask her just to pass by the causeway. I'll ask her hard to do that. Just so that you can see she is real. She'll be wearing a black hat with a purple feather, and she carries a stick with a gold handle. And she's got a dog called Bruce. You'll see all that when my Grandmother comes."

"Do you know something, Janie?" Gertie asked, anxious to make up for her unbelief. "That old bitch Beulah wasn't in a dwam at all. She just wasn't ill at all. Janie, she winked to me after you'd gone to beg tobacco for her."

Janie knew that now. And with the knowing, also knew that she didn't want to be a real tinker any more.

Chapter Five

THIS was the time to catch the Lane unawares. This early hour. Before day took over. The Lane still slept. Its grey face relaxed; a fine mist drifting up through the causeway mellowed its gaunt tenements. Soon the dustman's cart would clang and alarm the Lane into wakefulness, but now only furtive cats padded across its cobblestones.

Leaning from the high window at 285, Janie watched it all. Excitement had banished her sleep. More, her frock and her liberty bodice, washed in the dying minutes of the previous night, hung over the window-sill to dry. It wasn't the first time that Janie's sole wardrobe had fallen from this drying place on the window-sill into the gutter below. This was one time when no such risk could be taken. Today she was going to visit her Grandmother.

The rarity of a visit to Grandmother magnified it into a high occasion. And although such visits never lasted longer than a day, that one day encompassed so much that was strange to the Lane, that Janie looked on it with the apprehensive sense of seeing it for the last time.

Her liberty bodice still felt damp. That didn't

worry her, it could dry when it was on her, and nobody saw your liberty bodice anyhow. And, if the worst came to the worst, her print frock would dry in front of the gas-ring.

The first of the workers went clattering past now; then the bairns would follow with their pillowslips, in a great rush to Riley's back door to get the first chance of yesterday's loaves. Janie watched impatiently for a sight of Gertie. Like a genie, fretting to get out of his bottle to work his magic. It seemed so long in coming, that moment for shouting: "I'm off to see my Grandmother today, Gertie. Didn't I tell you last night that she was real?"

Last night Janie had arrived home, after her encounter with Beulah, to find her Mother home before her, sitting wiggling her toes and silently watching them wiggle; this was one of her Mother's "thinking" attitudes, so it wasn't really a surprise to Janie when her Mother stopped wiggling and announced abruptly: "I was thinking we'd go to see Grandmother the morn. A day away will do us both good. You'd better get your clothes off and nip into your bed, till I give them a wash through. You ought to have been home long since. Where did you get to till this time of night?"

"Just down to the Green. To Beulah's caravan."

"Not one word out of your head to your Grandmother the morn, about Beulah," Liza warned.

"God only knows what she'd think about you hobnobbing with all the tinkers in the town."

"Not a word, Mam," Janie agreed, struggling out of her bodice and beginning to share her Mother's anxiety over the visit. "There's only one button on my bodice. I always think Grandmother can see right through my frock to the lost buttons on my bodice."

"Hardly," Liza laughed. "Your Grandmother can see far, and deeper than most, but she just can't see through your frock. I'll stitch your bodice together when it's on you, tomorrow."

The bairns were running down the Lane now. Gertie stopped under the window. "Coming, Janie? Betsy's just got back from Riley's with loads of stale cakes with pink ice on them. We won't get none if we don't hurry."

"I can't." Loads of stale cakes with pink ice on them momentarily clouded Janie's other prospect. "I can't, Gertie. I'm standing here mother naked. All my clothes are washed."

"What are they all washed for?" Gertie shouted up curiously.

"Because I'm going to see my Grandmother today. That's what. If it's appletime at Grandmother's, I'll bring you back loads. There's hundreds of apple-trees."

"Come away from that window," Liza grumbled from the bed. "And pull it down, you're letting the draught in and I'm freezing. What time is it?"

"Gone seven. The mill hooter went a while back. It'll soon be time to go to Grandmother's."

"What like's the weather? If it promises rain, we'd maybe better bide at home," Liza said, beginning to regret the necessity of getting up so early.

"It's not raining, Mam." Janie was alarmed. "There's a mist. It's going to be a fine day. And you promised we'd go."

"Oh, all right. Fling over my corsets. They're under the chair somewhere." Anger crept into Liza's voice. "And my stockings, there! On the fender. It's the damned last time I'll promise anything."

Janie searched unbidden for her Mother's shoes and skirt, quietly, wordlessly. In moments like these it just took one word, one false move to wreck a promise.

The real business of going to see Grandmother had begun. Liza sat on a corner of the table counting the money in her purse. Janie, watching her, prayed silently: Let there be enough money for two train tickets. Please let there be enough money for the two of us. If not, I'll have to hide under the carriage seat again and I'm afraid that the Ticket Man will catch me one day.

"There's enough for my ticket," Liza said. "You'll just have to hide under the seat. Or, maybe," she considered, looking out of the window, "maybe we could walk there, and have enough for both our train fares back."

62

Janie seized the alternative, before her Mother could change her mind.

"That's a good idea, Mam. If we walked we'd have enough for your tobacco then. You can smoke all the way to Grandmother, and sing *Rolling Home To Bonnie Scotland* all the way back in the train without having to worry about the Ticket Man."

"We'd better get on our road then," Liza agreed, still looking out of the window. "It's a sea mist that's in it. Mist from the hill brings grist to the mill. But mist from the sea brings honey to the bee."

It was spring along the road to Grandmother's country. Not the dusty, daffodiled, yellow spring that Janie glimpsed on the barrows in High Street, but a spring that was sharp and white. Star of Bethlehem flowers clustered together in groups, like milestones flashing along the way. Hawthorn wound itself in thorny whiteness, smelling like heart-break, if heart-break could smell. The great fir wood of Laveroch shadowed the road; yellow primroses and blue vetch lost their own colour in its shadow, pale, like the wood's own wild, white anemones drifting down the banks.

"This is Grandfather's wood, isn't it, Mam?" Janie knew the answer, but wanted to hear it all again.

"Aye. Every inch of it," Liza said, wanting to

tell it all again. "There's no one so acquaint with a tree as your Grandfather. He can tell if it's in good heart just by listening to it. When I was little, I used to think he could speak to the trees."

"He never speaks to me," Janie remembered. "Not once ever. He just looks at me."

"That's his way," Liza said casually. "He seldom spoke to us as children. And we never spoke to him until we were spoken to."

"Was he a wild man, then?" Janie asked, thinking it very possible that he was.

"No. Your Grandfather never lifted his hand or voice to any of us in anger in his life. It was never necessary. A look from him was enough."

"Was Grandmother afraid of a look?"

"Never her." Liza laughed. "Your Grandmother could manage him. She always knew the right moment to speak. That was all that was to it. And Grandmother knew it."

"I like Grandmother best," Janie said decidedly. "Did you like her best when you was little, Mam?"

"No, Janie. I was Grandfather's favourite. He tried not to show it. But you just always know when you're somebody's favourite. I was always Miss MacVean to Grandfather. 'Where's Miss MacVean?' he'd shout, when he led the men and horses home. He'd lift me up beside him and I'd ride home on the first horse as proud as anything. We'll take the short cut through the wood now,"

Liza concluded abruptly. "Mind your feet jumping that ditch."

Janie wondered at her Mother's easy intimacy with this country; her quick recognition of the flowers in the woodworkers' gardens, with names unheard of in the Lane; Snow in Summer, Dead Man's Bells, Love in a Mist, Thyme, yellow St John's Wort, pink-starred bramble-blossom. "There's going to be a good crop of brambles the year." Liza cast an experienced eye over them. "We'll need to come for a day in autumn for the bramble picking." They wouldn't of course. But Janie had learned to enjoy the prospect more than the reality.

The wood thickened and dimmed. Great patches of wild hyacinths waved darkly blue. The sky was crowded out. Moss sprang beneath their feet, and the dust of it rose like thin smoke. The foosty guff of an ancient wood drifted over and past in great imprisoning waves. The Hangman's Tree loomed high in this dark heart of things. "Tell me all about it again, Mam," Janie pleaded, fearful but fascinated.

Liza, in one of her rare, enchanting moods, willingly complied:

> *There was a man that wadna' hang*
> *Three times upon a tree.*
> *Three times they strung him up aloft*
> *But never hang wad he.*

"Why couldn't they hang the man, Mam?"

Janie kept the question till well away from the darkness of the Hangman's Tree.

"I'm not sure." Liza considered carefully. "It may be, you know, that he was so bad a man that even the Devil didn't want him."

But there were others, less wicked, who had hanged on the gallows tree. MacPherson was one. The fiddler. "And anyone that had music as deep as he had couldn't be all that bad, with the exception of your Father of course, Janie. And there was none badder than him." Burns told of how MacPherson had gone to the Tree. You could hear MacPherson's fiddle in the way Burns told of it:

> *Sae rantingly, sae wantonly, sae dauntingly*
> *Gaed he.*
> *He played a spring and danced it round,*
> *Beneath the Gallow Tree.*

Those rare moods of communication between Janie and her Mother more than made up for the other things lacking in their relationship. And yet, if these moments had never existed, it would have been so much easier for Janie in the years to come.

Meanwhile the path through the wood widened. The sky pierced its way through the trees again; hyacinths blazed truly blue. And the light of the world outside the wood surprised the eye with momentary blindness. Primroses took on their own colour again, and vetch shouted in masses along the bank.

Grandmother's house stood high and red as Janie had remembered it. Where the sky met the fields marked the end of the world. But Grandmother's house stood safely in the centre, looking down over all the world. And all the world looked up and saw Grandmother's house.

"We're nearly there," Liza warned, tucking her pipe down the leg of her stocking. "That's the men yoking their horses. Thank goodness, Grandfather's had his dinner."

"If he's had dinner there might be none left for us," Janie said, alarmed at this prospect.

"There'll be plenty left for us in the pot," Liza assured her, "only, it's easier. Grandfather won't go without his dinner now."

"Why would Grandfather have to go without his dinner?" Janie asked curiously. "If there's plenty in the pot."

"Not from necessity," Liza answered. "From choice just. Once anyone does anything wrong to Grandfather, he never sits down at table nor breaks bread with them again."

"We didn't do anything wrong to Grandfather," Janie protested. "I've never even spoken to that man!"

"He thinks we did."

"Grandmother takes her tea with us then?"

"Grandmother sees things differently. If she didn't, Janie, I can assure you we wouldn't be walking up her roadway this day."

The last steps to Grandmother were harried

67

with last-minute warnings: "Mind now! Say please and thank you, Janie. Don't blow on your broth if it's too hot. Just have patience till it cools. And say 'No, thank you' if Grandmother offers you a second helping. Don't be gorging into you as if you hadn't seen food for days. And giving me a red face. And give your nose a good blow. And not sniff, sniff, sniff into your bowl all the time. And come here till I give your face a dicht. It always gets as black as the Earl of Hell's waistcoat."

The last and most important warning came more slowly and more clearly: "And, for the love of God, Janie, don't be asking to look inside your Aunt Morag's box."

"It isn't a box," Janie pointed out. "It's a treasure chest, Mam. Aunt Morag's got beads and hankies and pencils and scent and books. And she never gives me one of them."

The white flowers were coming out on the Butcher's Broom. Liza stood amongst them, explaining carefully: "Your Aunt Morag is a poor thing. She hasn't got a treasure chest at all. She's got a box. That's all it is, a brown box. And all the things she has inside it are just things her brothers and sisters gave her, because they're sorry for her. And mind, don't you go asking her to open that box. Because you won't get anything out of it."

"She's just greedy then," Janie concluded, pushing her way through Butcher's Broom, with

68

its faint, bitter smell. "And I hate my Aunt Morag."

"She's a poor thing," Liza said in her voice that you never argued with. "And don't you forget that."

It was dim in Grandmother's kitchen. The uncles' long, sprawling legs broke up the pattern of her red stone floor. Grandfather sat in his corner chair, his face hidden behind a newspaper. Aunt Morag in her wheelchair, sat staring out of the window, not turning her head to look upon the visitors.

The first dimness passed. The eyes sought out familiar brightness; the glinting brass-work on Aunt Morag's treasure chest the shining top of Grandmother's bellows; the gleaming face of the wall clock, ticking away the timelessness of this wait on the threshold.

"You've got here, then?" Grandmother's voice startled the uncles' long legs into their right places; the floor lay clear and red and patterned. Aunt Morag turned her head to stare on the visitors and looked away out of the window again. Grandfather stayed hidden behind his paper, and Grandmother bustled into a noise. "Sit you both down then. You'll be tired after your long travel." Her black apron rustled, so stiffly starched that it could have stood on the floor by itself without Grandmother being inside it at all. Liza found her voice and talked through the new, comforting noise.

"We thought we'd be better of a day away. A neighbour of ours died last week. Sudden kind. Janie and herself were very thick. And, to tell the truth, I felt a bit lost myself. We were so used to her."

"Poor soul," Grandmother said. "What would have ailed her like?"

"Nobody was rightly sure," Liza answered. "Some said this and others said that, but no one was sure."

It's Mysie Walsh Mam's telling of, Janie realised with surprise. But it wasn't like that at all, she thought excitedly. I could tell Grandmother all about it and what it was like. Something in the atmosphere prevented Janie from doing so; words that you volunteered got lost here, somehow, drifted up out of you, foundered in the air, and hurried back to the safety of your secret self again. Perhaps it all sounded best the way her Mother was telling it. Unreal. Just as the Lane and Mysie Walsh seemed unreal and far away in this kitchen.

"No man knows his dying hour," Grandmother said, never dreaming that Mysie Walsh had chosen her own hour. "And that's a true mercy. I'll away to the milk house for a bowl of buttermilk for the quean, it'll put body in her, till the broth comes to the boil again."

Grandmother took away with her the large safety she had thrown over the kitchen:

"She's no' at her school the day, then?" Uncle Hugh spoke for the first time.

"You can see that she's no'," Liza answered shortly.

"She'll never be a scholar." Grandfather's paper rustled in sharp agreement with Uncle Hugh. But Grandmother had returned, filling the kitchen with her tall self, and darkening the sun each time she passed the window.

"Come in about to the table now." And soon Grandmother was throwing all Liza's careful forewarnings to the wind: "Sup up now, Janie. Just you blow on your broth if it's a bit on the hot side. There's plenty more where that came from. Sup up, now. Never mind your Mother nudging you under the table there. Your belly maun be gey teem after your travel." Grandmother's voice rose roughly and comfortably. Soon Grandfather and the uncles would go out to Laveroch Wood with their horses, leaving a legacy of freedom behind them. Freedom to explore the milk house, dark and cool, with its great, stone slabs, its bowls of yellow cream, basins of brown hens' eggs and green ducks' eggs, its pale, shining rhubarb laid out on green leaves; its smell of an imprisoned summer, grass and clover and cold well water.

Freedom to peep into the "best" room, curtained against the light of day, its willow-pattern plates behind doors of glass, its chairs standing as if they had stood so for a hundred years. The piano that set up a quivering wail of protest when

71

you ever so quietly pressed one of its yellow keys, and all the whiskered men and ringleted ladies on the photographs above stared down in silent reproach. "When Grandmother first got the piano," Liza once told Janie, "she was so excited about it till Grandfather and the men came home at night to carry it into the house. She sat and played it under the trees; all the wood-workers got great fun out of that, but Grandmother didn't care, and she sat and played all afternoon. We children thought the world had come to an end, it was such an odd thing for Grandmother to do. She was always so tall and strict and busy."

Janie loved this picture of her Grandmother. Her piano had known the wood once and had made music for it. Now the wood was shut out with great, green curtains, and the piano had grown grumbling and old.

The uncles looked as if they would sit forever, till Grandmother got her broom and furiously swept amongst their feet. Her busyness shamed the long men into going. Their going stirred up the quick smell of fir resin and loam. For a moment the kitchen might have been Laveroch Wood itself.

"I'm away to throw the hens some corn," Grandmother said casually. "I'll maybe have a look in bye the black pig too. Anybody like to come?"

Janie jumped at the invitation. Inside the house Grandmother was old and very wise, knowing the

72

best cure for this ailment, and the worst weather for that ailment. Knowing what Paul had said to the Corinthians. And what someone ought to say very soon to that Geordie Scobie for underpaying country folk and overcharging town folk for their eggs. Outside the house was a different matter altogether. No ailments existed round the garden, out by the steading or in the wood. No one cared what Paul had said to the Corinthians. According to Grandmother when she got outside, Paul had once said something quite different:

> *Paul said and Peter said*
> *And all the saints alive and dead*
> *Swore she had the sweetest head,*
> *Bonnie, bonnie Bride of the yellow, yellow hair.*

Grandmother knew that the secret of her other self was safe in the keeping of the black pig and Janie. Neither of them thought it in any way odd for Grandmother to kilt up her apron and trip sedately round the sty to her own singing:

> *And she slept for a hundred years,*
> *Years, years.*
> *And she slept for a hundred years,*
> *A hundred years.*
> *Till Prince Charming came and kissed her*
> *Long ago.*

They stepped easily into this other world, the child and the Grandmother. Pondering over a new word for meadow. Muskoday. Musk in the

73

garden now. And small, yellow musk roses waiting to come in summer. High afternoon, the stable
doors open, the stables empty. No great, black
wood horses there now, to flick their tails, and
stamp their feet, and roll their wild and searching
eyes round a visitor. The whitewashed byre, dark
stone drinking troughs. An intruding hen whirred
out of her nest in the manger, cackling her resentment, and rousing the sleeping afternoon. "We'll
go in bye now," Grandmother said, "I'll make a
baking of scones for our tea. You can have a hot
one with milk. Hot scones are ill for the belly they
say, but I never died of eating one yet. And, for
an ill thing, a hot scone's got an unco fine taste."

The bellows roared the fire into redness.
Grandmother, huge and hurried in her white
baking apron, had become old and wise again.
Aunt Morag, still and quiet by the window,
shaded her face with her thin hands and lifted
her damp hair from her forehead. Only her eyes
had life in them. Blue. Like the sharp blue flames
that shot up through the fire, when Grandmother
threw salt in it to guard against ill-luck. The fire-
light glimmered along the brass work on Aunt
Morag's treasure chest.

"Can I see all your treasures again, Aunt
Morag?" Grandmother coughed harshly through
Janie's sudden request. Liza creaked in her chair,
and mentioned some flower that Janie had yet to
see. "Please, Aunt Morag, just one more look."

Aunt Morag smiled her first, small smile. Her

74

eyes became more brightly blue, her great box creaked open, lovingly and separately she took out its contents, holding them up against the light of the sun. Beads that flashed. Scent bottles blue and green and yellow, their scent remaining forever secret. Books with vivid jackets, pencils, and the blue bird brooch with pearls flashing on its wings. Soon the table was as crowded and coloured as the stalls in the Green. "I only want the blue bird brooch," Janie thought, staring at them all. "Just the blue bird brooch, but if I don't get that, I'd like anything else at all."

"Get that litter off the table, Morag," Grandmother commanded, roughly and fiercely. "I want to get the tea set up." Janie watched Aunt Morag return each treasure to its own corner of the box, her face pink, her eyes triumphant. The lid clanged down with ominous finality. And Janie's hopes clanged with it. Aunt Morag looked white once more, her hair damper than ever, and her eyes sought and held the window again.

Grandmother's voice sounded fiercer than ever: "Heaven only knows why you keep tormenting yourself with that box, bairn. You know fine there's nothing in it to spare for you. Or for anyone else. Come on and see if Grandmother's got something for you. And it's high time you were getting out of the sun for a while, Morag, you're taking up all the light."

Grandmother wheeled Aunt Morag into a corner, the geraniums stood revealed now, on the white window-sill, the light caught and danced across the row of Aunt Morag's medicine bottles. Janie turned and followed Grandmother, not even worried about the sharp, sly kick Liza gave her in passing. Aunt Morag was in disgrace. And Janie was glad.

"Haste ye back now, soon," Grandmother's voice came to them all the way past Butcher's Broom. Liza lit up her pipe with a great sigh of relief. It was good to be going back to the Lane again. Grandmother's country was frightening in the dusk. Wheeling curlews cried out in their loneliness. Wood cushats grumbled in their sleep, flapping crows screamed in last angers. Janie ran on in front to have a Think, and having thought, relayed it all to Liza:

"Mam, I wish the man that owns Woolworth's would give me the biggest sack in the world, and let me choose all the things I wanted off his counters. I'd fill the sack as full as anything. With beads and books and scent and things. I'd show every one of them to Aunt Morag. Then I'd put them all back in my sack again and not give her one thing. That's an awful good Think, isn't it?"

Liza took the pipe from her mouth and stared at Janie. "That's just about the wickedest Think I've ever heard tell of," she said. "Just the wickedest. If Grandmother knew you'd think like that,

76

she'd never give you eggs and butter and jam to take home with you again."

"But that's what Aunt Morag does to me," Janie insisted.

"Nothing of the kind, Janie," Liza said with finality. "Your Aunt Morag's a chronic invalid. Don't you forget that." Liza put her pipe in her mouth again, the smell of it rose homely and comfortingly in the air. The lights of Kinloch Station twinkled in the distance. Janie was glad there was enough money to take the train home.

Chapter Six

THE morning after the visit to Grandmother possessed no time in its own right. It became this time yesterday on the road to Grandmother's house, or this time tomorrow when I'm back at school, and my name's on the register again. It became any time at all, except its immediate, worrying self.

"Janie had a bad cold and couldn't come to school," Liza scribbled hurriedly. That this was a lie didn't worry Janie. That Teacher would know it was a lie worried her exceedingly.

"Hurry up, Janie. You'll be late today, as well as absent yesterday." Liza, too, had morning-after regrets. "Take this rhubarb in bye to Betsy in your passing. We haven't got the right pot for it. Get a move on. It's nearly ten to nine. And don't be standing there sniffing at the rhubarb. It hasn't got any smell."

But it had. A smell of yesterday. Of Grandmother's milk house. A small, intangible smell of far-off safety.

The line to Teacher lay on a corner of her table. Janie kept her eyes fixed on *High Summer*, the huge painting on the opposite wall. Staring at it with the desperate singlemindedness of shutting out all other sights. Especially the line to Teacher on the corner of the table. Any moment now, Miss Sim would say:

"Janie MacVean, take this line to the Headmaster."

High Summer, blazing down from the wall, withheld the moment in a great maze of greenery.

A voice more ominous than the voice of Miss Sim broke through *High Summer*. Janie saw the startling figure of Nurse Conduit in the doorway, her list of Names To Be Examined in her hand.

Janie's first impulse was to shoot her hand up in the air: "Please, Miss Sim, may I leave the room?" And rush through the door and away out of the schoolgates altogether. But that means of escape from Nurse would have been too obvious. It wouldn't have worked.

Other means of escape crowded swiftly in on Janie. It wasn't Nurse Conduit who stood in the doorway at all. It was Mr Thompson, the Headmaster, smiling and hurried. "Excuse me, Miss Sim," he said, "but I would like to speak to my daughter for a moment, if you don't mind."

"Certainly, Mr Thompson," Miss Sim replied, all pink and puzzled. "Children, the Headmaster would like to speak to his daughter. Where is she?"

Everybody got a great surprise to discover that Janie was really the Headmaster's daughter all the time. Especially Gertie. She just stared with her mouth open when Mr Thompson put his arm round Janie's shoulder and led her away, saying very loudly: "Janie, my dear."

Now it was Grandmother, dressed in her Sunday clothes, who strode through the doorway, tut, tut, tutting Nurse and Miss Sim out of the way and making straight for Janie's desk, singing as she had sometimes sang in the black pig-sty:

> *Off we'll go to London Town,*
> *Yo Ho, my lads. Yo Ho, my lads.*
> *We'll see the King wi' the golden crown,*
> *Yo Ho, my lads. Yo Ho, my lads.*

Not knowing that this was just Grandmother's way, everybody in the class would think that Grandmother was really going to see the King and taking Janie with her. In her Sunday clothes Grandmother looked as if she could go anywhere at all.

"Janie MacVean." It was Nurse Conduit's voice that dispelled all images of escape. At least, thought Janie, as she walked forward to join the group of children on the floor, my frock's still clean from yesterday. So is my bodice. And I haven't got knickers to worry about. But I've still got nits in my hair. Nurse Conduit will be sure to find them. She always bone-combs my hair so well. She just flicks her fingers through other folks' heads. Lucky other folk, Janie thought, as she watched Connie Morne and Isla Skea and

Shona Coolin, whispering and laughing easily together, enjoying Nurse's visit as a break in lessons. Shona Coolin, that's a lovely name for such a horror to have. She never once lends me her rubber. My name's Shona too. My real name. Only it's Grandmother's name as well. But Grandfather will never let us use it. So I've got to be called Janie instead. It's the English name for mine. Janie. A terrible name.

"Gertie Latham." Nurse Conduit's voice brought a gleam of comfort. Janie wouldn't, now, be de-loused alone. More, they both had the secret of "nits" to keep together from the rest of the children.

"It isn't fair," Janie confided to Gertie later, "everybody in the class must know that we've got nits. That stuff Nurse put on our heads smells terrible. It makes my head itch all over. And I think I'll kill that Connie Morne if she goes on sniffing the smell out loud and laughing and whispering about us."

It was a mystifying day. Nurse hadn't given Janie a note to take home to her Mother. "And that's a funny thing, Gertie. Because you've got one. And I always get one too."

Nor was any word spoken about the line for being absent. Not even by the Headmaster when he came into the class-room. He seemed quite unaware of the existence of his "daughter". The news he brought was momentous.

"You all belong to a city with the oldest and

loveliest Cathedral in Scotland. I'd like to discover just how much you all know about the subject. To the pupil who writes the best essay on the Cathedral, I'm going to award a prize of one shilling. Find out all you can about it. Better still, go down to see it, and tomorrow you'll write your essays."

"That bob's mine for certain," Janie informed Gertie, without conceit. "My Mam knows everything about history, if I can just catch her in the mood for telling."

Liza *was* in the mood for telling. "We're off to see some old friends of ours. Quiet folk down bye," she said cryptically to Poll, as herself and Janie walked through the causeway. "You see, the dead that lie in the Cathedral are awful quiet folk, Janie," she explained, twinkling, when they were out of Poll's hearing. "But of course we don't tell Poll that, we just leave her guessing."

Janie had often seen the Cathedral looming darkly through the trees. It stood close by the Green. In summer charabancs drew up in front of it. Flower-frocked women stared at it from beneath large hats, clicked their cameras, and made their way to the fair on the Green. Old women of the city drowsed beneath the Cathedral's trees. They knew every inch of the Green and every aspect of the Cathedral, and the time for staring at both was over. Old men pottered and bent amongst the Cathedral's tombstones, then they too sheltered and slept beneath its trees. In Janie's mind the Cathedral was a resting place for the old, and a thing of curiosity for the stranger. Until now. Until Liza gave it a vivid, personal life of its own, and Janie began to see it through her Mother's most curious eyes.

"The Wolf of Badenoch, swooping down from the high hills behind Forres. The clang of his horses' hoofs ringing on the cobbles, wakening the sleeping townsfolk and sending them scurrying out into the streets, curious and frightened. Their curiosity diminished but their fear heightened when they saw the flames rise red and high from the airt of the Cathedral. The whole town was alow, Janie. Everybody in the world must have known where our town lay, with the red sky of fire that was above it. Quiet monks in brown cassocks chanting their queer, Latin words on this very spot, maybe. Hearing the nearing noise of the Wolf and his men. But like as not the monks had gone on singing till they came to the end of their song. The burning torches, the flash of skean dhus, the cries of the wounded, an old monk hiding beneath a tree, watching the Cathedral blacken and crumble and fall all round him, knowing that it would be built again, but he would be too old to have part in it again. And unco sad in heart at the knowing. The plunder over, the destruction done, the Wolf of Badenoch clattering out of the town again. His loot lighting up the darkness; golden chalices and silver crucifixes. Townsfolk lurking in the shadows, crossing themselves at the devilish departure of holy things. And, mind you, Janie, I've not got muckle meed for Popish things. But it was the first, old faith of our land. Though your Grandfather will never allow mention of that. His religion lay in a chield by name of John Knox. Him that put the clampers down on Mary Queen of Scots. She was Queen of Bonnie France. But that's a story for some other time. And, Papes or no Papes, the monks were fine craftsmen. You've only got to look at this Cathedral to see the truth of that. They gave our Lane its name too. Our Lady's Lane. They must have walked through it often, and been byordinar fond of it, to give it a name like that. You wouldn't think it to see the Lane now. But maybe it was all different four hundred years ago."

"It's different sometimes now," Janie remembered. "But you've got to see it early in the morning, when it's all misty, to catch the difference."

"Just one last thing," Liza said, as they made their way out of the Cathedral, through the tombstones. "It's hard to tell whether the Bishops and Archbishops all lying here were good men or bad, because all that's told about them is written in Latin. But here's a stone that I like. Everybody can understand it. Listen to it, Janie:

Here lies Martin Elginbrod,
Have mercy on my soul, Lord God,
As I would have, were I Lord God,
And You but Martin Elginbrod.

A fine man that," Liza concluded, closing the gate of the Cathedral behind them. "And mind you, Janie, hurry home with my shilling for the essay the morn."

"There was a man looking for you, Liza," Poll greeted them, when they arrived back at the Lane. "I didn't see him myself, but wee Lil here was speaking to him. He came back and fore three times."

"It was the Cruelty Man," wee Lil broke in, "asking me questions about you and Janie, there. But I'm not the one to meddle with my neighbours' affairs. He got small change out of me," Lil ended quickly, frightened by the sudden tallness and glint that had come over Liza.

"He couldn't get much out of you, could he, Lil?" Liza burned Lil up in a look. "Nor from you either, Poll." Her anger extended itself to Poll. "Because none of you know anything about Janie and me. Do you, now? Except, of course, the kind of things that would interest the Cruelty. And I bet you let him have the lot. I bet you did. You'd have licked his boots all right, and would have licked his arse too, if your tongue had been a bit longer."

Liza strode up to 285, declining Janie's company. "You run and play yourself for a while."

"She's a dark horse that, and no mistake," Poll condoled with wee Lil. "I can't make her out at all. But you'll see, she won't get herself out of this lot. She's lost that Janie. It'll be a Home for her. Or my name's not Poll Pyke."

"And the bairn would be better in a Home," wee Lil agreed. "She'd be sure of a bite and a sup. And God only knows there can be no example for a bairn up at 285. There's no' much of a life for any bairn in the Lane, if it comes to that."

If Janie had heard Lil's sentiments she would have been entirely out of agreement with them. The Lane was home and wonderful. And even more home and more wonderful in moments like these, when it seemed at stake. A long line of men drifted out of the Labour Exchange, throwing their usual sallies over to the women in the causeway: "Where's your Ramsay MacDonald now, Poll?"

"Up my clothes," Poll flung back in kindred mood.

"By God, he'll get fair lost there, then, Poll."

Their rising laughter covered Janie's apprehension. A group of bairns, showing off, chanted their ball game on the cobbles:

> *One, two, three a-leerie,*
> *Four, five, six a-leerie,*
> *Seven, eight, nine a-leerie,*
> *Ten a-leerie. Postman!*

"I've been looking for you all over, Janie," Gertie's voice broke through the noises. "Where did you get to?"

86

"Down to the Cathedral for the essay," Janie said quickly, for the essay no longer seemed important. "I think I'll have to go away to a Home," she added, partly to shock Gertie, and partly to put her own apprehension into real words. "Cruelty Man was looking for me. He was up here three times."

"That's nothing." Gertie remained disappointingly unshocked. "Cruelty Man's often up at our house. He looks through all the blankets, then inside the cupboards, and if he catches you he looks in your head as well. He's never catched me. My Dad bawls him out of it. Come on, Janie, I've something to show you down High Street. There's going to be a ball in the Assembly Rooms. They're all lit up. And there's a new frock in your shop. But the frock's mine because I saw it first."

Down High Street took the edge off apprehension. Gertie and Janie "owned" many of the shops in High Street. Ownership of the same being acquired by merely being first to reach and touch a shop window, laying the formal vocal claim: "My Shop." Janie's proudest property was a small dress shop, which only displayed one dress at a time, a grown-up, Cinderella creation, at which Janie and Gertie would stare, snub-nosed and appreciative, seeing themselves so adorned in the miraculous, but far-off time of grown-upness. Today, the dress in the window surpassed its predecessors. It was white, glowing and glimmering with silver sequins. Passing girls stopped to look at it, oh-ing and ah-ing in little groups, edging the children away, to get a better look, never dreaming that Janie owned the shop and Gertie owned the white dress because she had seen it first.

Down at the Assembly Rooms, the lights lit up the street, dancers flitted past the windows, sudden whirls of bright colour. The music drifted down to those watching from the street. *When You and I Were Seventeen*. Some of the girls sang the words, some of them waltzed on the pavements to the tune, the policeman edging them away, to let the lawful dancers pass through. A new distraction arrived on the scene. Forty Pockets, with his barrel organ and his monkey in its bright red petticoat. Janie and Gertie, delighted to see him, forsook their hard-won position with its view of the Ball. The music from the barrel organ drowned out the music from the Ball. Back to the land where the skies are so blue. Please give the monkey a penny, too.

"Move along," the policeman shouted. "No obstruction here, now. Keep moving, all of you."

"And don't you follow us," Gertie threatened some children from a rival lane. "Because Forty Pockets is more ours than yours. Him and the monkey stays in the next Lane to us."

"Beat it," Forty Pockets snarled, unmoved by Gertie's loyalty. "Don't you two be trailing after me all night." The monkey stared at them brightly, his red bonnet on one side, his red petticoat hanging on one side too.

"I bet you Forty Pockets beats that poor monkey," Gertie said as they ran towards the Lane. "And he smells terrible with all that dirty old coats he's got on. No wonder everybody calls him Forty Pockets."

Back at the Lane the children bounced their ball to a perpetual chant. A week ago they had skipped to *A big Ship Came to the Eelie, Ilie O*. Next week they would be running round in rings to *She is the Girl of the Golden City*. But no chant ever overstepped its own mysterious season, and this week it would be a bouncing ball and *One, Two, Three A-Leerie*.

"Can Gertie and me get a game?" Janie asked the owner of the ball, formally, as strict etiquette in the matter of street games required.

"If you take the last turn," the ball owner answered, "because you two joined in last."

To be a leader in street games required not so much personal ability, as personal possessions. The owner of a ball or a skipping rope invariably got off to a good start in the race for being "Boss". Janie had savoured the powers of leadership for brief spells, usually broken by some irate mother: "You and your bloody Ghost in the well! My Rosanna didn't get a wink of sleep last night." You had to be very humble when you were not the Boss of a game. The least unwitting word of criticism brought forth the dreaded and irrevocable judgment: "Out of this game, You. It's my ball."

There were rare moments, though, needing much self-denial, when you could take the initiative first, and shout: "I'm not playing. It's just a lousy game." More, the Boss of a game could always cheat and get away with it, saying that it was a bad turn of the rope or that the ball was thrown too low, too high, too fast or too slow. This you patiently endured for the sake of getting your turn. When your turn was over you could get your own back by deliberately throwing the ball too hard, too fast, too high all at the same time and getting the Boss "accidentally" but firmly in the place where it hurt her most.

Janie seldom resorted to such brutal methods: she had a more subtle and effective method of dealing with the Boss: "I know a game. A new one. You don't have to wait your turn, you can all play at once. Who's coming to my game?"

They all came, of course, lured by the promise of an equal share, except the Boss of the previous game. "And you can't come," Janie would inform her, becoming as much of a Boss herself, as the Bosses she thought she despised. "You can't come, because this is *my* game."

When your turn was last, as Janie's turn was now, no such tactics were practicable. The game might end long before your turn came, and then, of course, it wouldn't matter. On the other hand if the game didn't end, you didn't want to ruin your chance of a turn. In those eternities of being "last" Janie stared at the walls of the causeway and at the cobbles round her feet so long and hard that, in after years, she could still recall the patterns of cracks on the walls and the shapes of the cobble-stones in the Lane. Meantime, the voices of the Lane's women drifted through and over the chant of the ball game.

"I can tell you one thing," the Duchess was affirming, "and I'll tell you it for nothing. If this strike goes on, they won't be sitting so cooshy on their thrones. I heard Nelly's Bert vow just the other day that he'd tear Royalty to bits with his own two bare hands. And you know what Bert's like when he's in a paddy. And he's been in a paddy all right since the tweed mills had to close down. What's more, he's off now on the hunger march to London."

"You can never tell what will happen," Poll marvelled, as if Nelly's Bert might both end the strike and "do" the Royal family the moment he arrived in London. "If the mines don't start up by winter, we'll all die off like flies."

"It's bad enough," the Duchess agreed, "when you haven't got the price of a bag of cinders, but it's even worse when there's no cinders to be got, even though you haven't the price of them. It's them not being there that gets you down."

"My Hugh's old man won't last through another winter," Poll cheered up. "I can see him failing under my eyes. Mind you, he's had a good innings. And I'm not going to pretend I'm sorry he's going. There'll be more room left for the rest of us. I've put up with a lot from the old cove. But it's his spitting and slavering all over that I just can't abide. It's all on account of his catarrh. But still, you forget that when you've got to clean up after him."

"Do you know something?" the Duchess broke in, with the eagerness of discovery. "It's just a week tomorrow since Mysie Walsh did for herself. And, by God, I haven't had time to miss her yet."

"It all happened so quick," Poll agreed. "That you still kind of expect her to come jazzing through the causeway, acting the goat, the way she used to."

"My Mother went off sudden," wee Lil recalled. "It was her heart though. One moment she was as living like as you, Poll. She'd been down to the Ham Factory for a tanner's worth of pigs' trotters. It was a Saturday. We always had pigs' trotters on Saturday. She got home with them, slumped down on her chair, and died there and then. I've never been able to eat pigs' trotters since. What with the shock and one thing and another, the worry of getting all her relations on the spot for the funeral, and getting the Insurance money from her death policy to bury her, for she'd got a week or two behind with her payments. And you know what like the Insurance are when you're a bit behind. Especially if you die. Though God knows she'd paid it regular for over thirty years, enough to bury three folk. And what with Pinner the undertaker, and you know him. Has to see the colour of his money first, before he measures you. No cash and you can keep your corpse. And scurrying around everywhere looking for a cheap bit of black, since I was chief mourner, of course. My Mother was buried for weeks before I realised she was really dead. I picked up her coat one day, it smelled all of her. That was the first time I knew she was dead and gone. I cried terrible when it came home to me."

"Death's always worse when it hits sudden," the Duchess assured them. "Because it just gives you a wee push at first, then it gets tore right into you and knocks you flat on your face."

"You can have the rest of my turn, Janie. My Mam's shouting me. I'm at 'Open the gates, and let me through, Sir'."

The rare thing had happened in the street game, an accidental and "preferred" turn. "Janie's got to get the rest of my turn," Maikie Stewart informed the Boss. "Because I've got to go. And I've just had half a turn. And that's fair, because I waited here for ages."

The game came to a standstill, while the legal aspects of such an infrequent contretemps were debated.

"That's fair enough," Poll suddenly refereed

the squabble that had arisen, threatening to become a free-for-all, from the vantage point of her grown-upness. "It's fair enough. If you're due a thing and can't take it yourself, you can hand your due over to anybody you name."

"All right," the Boss agreed reluctantly, her personal wishes thwarted by such a powerful adversary as Poll, but still holding on to some of her dignity of office. "But Gertie Latham still has to wait till last for her turn."

Gertie didn't have to wait till last. But neither she nor anybody else knew that, as Janie caught the ball for her turn.

One, two, three a-leerie.

"Not from the beginning, Janie! Maikie did that." The squabble rose renewed. "You've only got half a turn. It's from 'Open the gates'."

Open the gates, and let me through, Sir
Open the gates.

The causeway was very quiet. Even the women had a sudden interest in this controversial turn. The watchful quietness unnerved Janie. The end of the chant seemed so far away:

Open the gates, and let me through, Sir
Open the gates.

"The ball's down. Janie dropped the ball at 'Open the gates'. She's out. She just went and dropped it." The cries rose through the causeway

94

in mingled accents of triumph and regretfulness. Gertie's voice rising in admonishment. "Getting to 'Open the gates' and going and dropping it, Janie. Your turn's gone now."

"I meant to drop it," Janie informed them, "because I'm needing the lavatory in a hurry. Gertie can have the rest of my turn," she cried as she flew up the causeway. An argument which not even Poll had the power to settle rose fierce and furious behind her. But Janie flew beyond it all, as if compelled, to the lobby of 285. Only to the lobby, apprehensive of her Mother's reception of this most urgent question.

"Mam," she shouted up the stairs. "Will you die soon?" And lest the answer should be in the dreaded affirmative, added: "Just say this one time that you won't die soon."

The answer, when it came, was hurried and irritable.

"I don't know when I'll die. For goodness' sake run and play."

Janie didn't. She stood for a long time in the lobby, getting her face quiet and ordinary again, to meet the other bairns. It took a long time to get your face ordinary so that no one would know anything had happened. And, in the longness, Liza's voice came down again, with laughter and assurance in it: "Of course I won't die soon. What on earth would I do going and dying?" Janie ran from the lobby, lest death should change its mind again.

"I thought you was off to the lavatory," Gertie was accusing. "Did you get a penny?"

"No. I had to go to speak to my Mam, that's all."

"You look as if you'd got a penny or something." Gertie's suspicions were unallayed. And although Gertie was Janie's very best friend, Janie sensed that not even to Gertie could she confide the truth: "I've just got a promise from my Mam that she won't die soon."

A promise that lit and warmed the Lane for the rest of the night, that put the apprehension of the Cruelty Man completely out of mind, that made Woolworth's bangles shine more brightly on the young girls' arms, that whirled herself and Gertie faster round the street lamp than ever, singing as they whirled:

> *We're two little piccaninnies,*
> *Real gems you know,*
> *We're the real dusky diamonds,*
> *Only from Iohio.*

Chapter Seven

THE worst had happened. Liza stared silently at the blue summons in her hands. She had sat there staring at it for a long time now, discovering from it that Janie was neglected, and in need of care and protection.

To Janie it seemed that Liza, numbed and white and bewildered, was really the one who needed care and protection. Janie found herself able to provide both.

"We'll go away, Mam. Miles and miles away together. Where nobody will ever find us. They can't take me away from you if they can't find us," she reasoned.

"They'd catch up on us sometime," Liza answered dully, but not dogmatically.

And Janie pressed her "prospect" home.

"Not for years and years, maybe. We could sell bowls and bootlaces, like Beulah does. Nobody worries about tinker children. So they wouldn't worry about us any more. Not if we become real tinkers."

"I know a place," Liza said tentatively. "It's a long walk from here. But I know we could get a cheap bed in this place."

It was dusk when they slipped together away

from the Lane. It was difficult to hear Liza say casually to Poll as they passed through the causeway:

"I've got one of yon heads of mine coming on. I thought we'd take a turn round the Green for a bit of air."

Difficult not to blurt excitedly out to Poll:

"We're really going away forever, Poll. You'll never see us again ever."

Difficult, because that was the only exciting bit of "news" they had ever had to impart to Poll.

Each familiar landmark loomed up in supplication of farewell. Janie said good-bye silently to the chip-shop and all the buildings that couldn't speak and report them to the police, and still gave them a sense of "belonging", till they reached the Toll Booth on the outskirts of the town.

"We're real tinkers at last," Janie thought, with a great sigh of relief, when they had passed through the gates.

The relief of being a real tinker communicated itself to Liza. She lit her pipe. The first "light up" for a long time.

The road they took was strange to Janie. "It leads to the next town," Liza explained. "There's a Diddle Doddle there. With a bit of luck, we'll get a bed for ninepence."

Janie lagged behind, eyeing the children playing round cottage doors, with a sense of triumph

98

and pity. They were confined to their doors, they weren't going on to "the next town". Passing carters grumbled good-night and rumbled out of sight up farm roads. Clusters of lights foretold another village, enclosing and cheering the travellers, letting go of them suddenly out into a darkness intensified by the remote glint of a lamp in an isolated farm house.

"I'll carry you on my back for a while," Liza offered, when the next four villages didn't turn out to be the "next town".

The darkness was more frightening from the height of Liza's shoulders than it was on the ground. Branches tugged at Janie's hair. The one shadow the two of them cast was taller than the trees themselves. A long hunchbacked stranger loping beside them.

"Let me down, Mam," Janie begged. "I'm not tired now. Honest I'm not."

"I can see the lights of the next town now," Liza said. "We'll be there in no time. And mind, Janie, when we reach the Diddle Doddle, we're just there because we missed our last bus home. And our name's Sinclair. Mind you don't forget that if you're asked any questions."

The Diddle Doddle was filled with light and noise and people. A hot plate glowed redly, sizzling with frying pans, the overpowering smell of onions tantalised hunger. Men spat on the sawdust on the floor. Women clattered enamel mugs on a table. Voices rose in laughter, song, oaths and temper. The owners of the voices were all vagrants. Janie instantly and warmly felt at home. An at-homeness which helped to cover Liza's bewildered lostness.

A small tinker mended dishes on the table, her slim, brown fingers controlled her whirring, whirling mending wheel, setting her eyes free to watch the ever-opening Diddle Doddle door. She seemed to know everyone who came through it, greeting them like an unofficial hostess who also happened to be a true friend. The rare combination lit her with charm.

"Strike me down stone dead, Mairi," she greeted a newcomer. "I thought you was bound for Mosstowie. The last time I saw your face it was set in the direction to Kinross. And is Lindsay with you this time at all, now?"

"Never him." The newcomer resignedly slung her pack on the table. "He got himself mixed up with some whoreson of a McPhee at New Pitsligo. They were all set up to hawk the Bullers of Buchan airt when I last saw them. And I'm no' sorry. I can tell you that, Aggie. I had my bellyfull of the breed of him."

"It's as I've always said, Mairi." Aggie's wheel purred round with contentment. "The road's always easier and faster when you take to it on your own. And there's always a man to be had when the need for one comes over you. But the need's not always over you. And, when it isn't, any cove's just a dead loss to you."

The Diddle Doddle dimmed down with heat. Thick pipe smoke curled round it, padding its noise into a hum. Its occupants looked as hazy and relaxed as Janie felt. Voices made the most comforting sounds in the world.

"You're going to cross water within a three, my dear."

A fortune teller peered down into Liza's tin mug.

"A sad crossing, my love. But you'll survive it. I can see that in your face, as well as in your leaves. There's a dark man here, too. He has crossed your life before. He's in your path again. Still after you."

"That's the Cruelty Man," Janie realised to herself. "He's got a great, big black moustache."

"This dark man has got an S in his name," the fortune teller continued. "You wouldn't recognise a man with an S in his name, would you, now?" she urged.

"It isn't the Cruelty Man." Janie turned away with relief. "He hasn't got an S. His name's F. Murray."

A man with no legs startlingly propelled himself through the door.

"It's the Railway Tramp," the Dish Mender shouted gladly. "Bless you, Thoomikies, my wee love. You all set for the Timmer Market too?"

The legless man grinned. A great, black hairy grin.

"Thoomikies is taking the short cut to the Market. Aren't you, old Cock? Nipping over the sleepers, and all round the junctions," a man teased. "And don't you fall asleep on the slag heap either. Old Thoomikies did that one night, and felt so burned up that he thought he was in Hell at last. Didn't you, son?"

The Diddle Doddle lifted up one voice and laughed. The Railway Tramp grinned in echo, squeezing himself compactly into the corner by the hot-plate and the wall, filling it so exactly that the room seemed only to be completely furnished at this moment. Janie stared at him fearfully. Their equal size brought their eyes level with each other. The tramp held a penny between his teeth, His great head nodded, beckoning Janie to come for the penny.

"Go on, Littl'un," the Dish Mender coaxed. "It will please Thoomikies terrible if you take his penny. He's fond of littl'uns, but they're all so feared of him."

But Janie couldn't. Not even to please Thoomikies. She turned frightenedly away from his eyes.

With the entrance of Blind Jimmy, the Diddle Doddle began to sing.

> *The summer's gone*
> *And all the flowers are dying.*

Led by Blind Jimmy, they all sang. As if in a sleep, their eyes closed, their bodies sagging across the table, or stretched in corners by the hot plate.

"He can sing like an angel," the Dish Mender said sadly, "especially when you consider that he hasn't got his sight. But for all that, Jimmy's a bit too free with his hands the moment he gets within an inch of a woman."

"Aye," the Fortune Teller agreed drily. "Blind or no' blind they always know their road in that direction."

But the blind street singer's voice transcended his natural instincts:

> *For I'll be there*
> *When summer's in the meadows.*
> *Or when the valley's hushed*
> *And white with snow.*

The entrance of two policemen with the Warden of the Diddle Doddle brought Danny Boy to a premature close. The singers loved the law too little to serenade it. They closed up, condensing themselves along the forms, busying their fingers with the tools of their trades. The policemen examined the backs of their heads, recognising one here and there:

"Been taking a turn through Balvenie woods lately, Joss?"

"No, Sergeant. To tell you the honest truth, I've gone kinda off rabbits these days. They don't agree with my digestion no more."

103

"You'll no' have gone off venison too, Joss?" the Sergeant asked heavily.

"I'm no' sure, Sergeant. It's so long since I've tasted a steak, that I forget if it speaks back to me now or no'."

"All signed in for the night, then?" the Sergeant turned to the Warden.

"Aye. Here's the book. House full the night. Most of them are moving on the morn, though."

"The Bobbies have come for me and Mam," Janie thought, afraid, watching the policeman gaze down on the signatures in the book. Her fear communicated itself to them. They looked down at her curiously.

"You're a bit on the young side for this game, are you no'?"

"She's mine," Liza said. "She's with me. We missed our last connection home."

The policeman stared down on the book again: "Is your name MacVean?"

"Yes," Liza answered with a voice that had no fear in it. "MacVean of Laverock."

"I thought we were Sinclairs now, Mam," Janie said, as they followed the Dish Mender and the other women up long stone steps to bed.

"I know, Janie. I shouldn't have told them who we were. But I just had to. It made me feel real for a minute just hearing to myself who I really was."

The Diddle Doddle folk said good-bye to each other in their good-nights:

"If I don't see you in the morning before I go, Aggie, I'll be catching up with you again at the Timmer Market."

"Aye. Or on the road to Foggie, maybe. I havena' hawked that road for years now."

Their reunions were chance. Their good-byes, being chance too, were without the regret that tinges ordinary good-byes:

"Good luck, Mairi, if you're on the road before me in the morning. I'm bound for the herring town myself. I hope to get there before the season starts up."

"Janie," Liza whispered, when the lights were out. "Are you sleeping yet, Janie? You and me are going to give ourselves up the morn."

Diddle Doddle life, wonderful to Janie, had frightened Liza more than the summons to court.

"The years will birl bye in a blink," Liza assured Janie, as they sat together in the ante-room of the Courthouse, waiting for the Vigilance Officer to come and take Janie to a Home.

"You've just got no idea how quick the years fly," Liza insisted, thereby also reassuring herself, as she sat there, carefully picking small digestible scraps off the bare bones of the Court's decision and handing them to Janie.

"The Home's a hundred miles away. Three hours' journey by train. The longest time you've ever been on a train. You're going to like that fine, Janie."

Liza's voice increased the desolation of those last moments together. The anteroom smelt sharp and clinical as all Janie's preconceived ideas of "a Home". Its austerity more fearful than any pool of blood that had ever incarnadined the Lane. Its silence more ominous than all the curses coursing through the causeway.

Liza, feeling the chill of the anteroom too, floundered through it, falling back on a more familiar facet:

"Poll and them fair got one in the eye. Thought all they had to do was to flock down to the Court and cock themselves up in the gallery, getting an eyeful of everything. But, no faith you. Nothing doing. They werena' even allowed a foot across the door. I bet you a pound to a penny though, they've all draped themselves along the railings outside. Just waiting to gape when you come out. And that's another shock in store for them. Like as not you'll be taken out by the side door."

Liza chuckled at the small triumph of it. And Janie was momentarily lifted out of bleakness into importance. I don't want to go out by the side door, she thought protestingly. I want them all to see me. I'll just cry and kick up something terrible, if they're all there looking.

The Lane's instinct both to provide and appreciate "a show" was deeply ingrained in Janie. Such a moment came only once to the children of the Lane. Like the time when the Probation Officer had to come to take Tom Shoggie to a Training Ship. How the Lane had lifted up its voice in lamentation:

"God help us all. Mind you, there's no gain-saying but that Tom was a bit on the wild side. Still, he was just Maggie Shoggie's craittur for all that."

One would miss one's epitaph completely, huddled out by a side door!

"The Home's in Aberdeenshire," Liza was saying. "Just a small home it is. Though all I can mind about Aberdeenshire is a hill called Lochnagar. There's a song to that hill:

> *O for the crags that are wild and majestic.*
> *I sigh for the valley of dark Lochnagar.*

The Home's in a place called Skeyne," Liza went on, "though I've never heard tell of Skeyne myself."

Skeyne. Janie turned the sound of the place round and over in her mind. It was familiar. Like the bed-cover that the Duchess crocheted on summer days. It had never reached an end in all the summers. Blue skeins. Yellow skeins. Red skeins. "All out of stock," the Duchess would grumble, "just when I needed skeins of that colour for my pattern." And the bright bed-cover would disappear, bereaving the causeway of colour. But, on some other summer day, it would blaze back to the causeway, shimmering and rippling against the Duchess's large bosom in triumphant folds. "I got the right skeins at last," she would inform the Lane. "And no' before time neither."

There was some magical quality to the Duchess's bright bed-cover. You felt it would never come to an end and turn into a real bed-cover. And all because of some elusive skein. Skeyne. Janie liked the sound of the place where the Home was.

Chapter Eight

SKEYNE never had the colour of its sound. It lay on the threshold of Deeside, a doormat against which hurrying tourists wiped their feet, their eyes straining ever forwards towards the greater glories of the Moor of Dinnet and Lochnagar. Skeyne lay sulking eternally under this slight, its grey face lined and loured with the perpetual shadow of the Cairngorm Mountains.

The Orphanage of Skeyne folds itself back from the main road, withdrawing into a huddle of trees. Tall trees, top-heavy and shaggy with crows' nests, loud with their rancour. Trees that shuddered and whined throughout Janie's first night in the Orphanage, twining their shadows across the walls of the dormitory.

It had been a long day. Still spring. But it seemed to have been spring in Grandmother's country ages ago. A white, quiet spring, then. Now it was loud and yellow. The glare of daffodils crowding out the Orphanage garden still beat hotly under Janie's heavy eyelids; the smell of them hovered through her senses. The suddenness of their impact had imprinted itself in her being. I'll never smell a daffodil in all my life again without minding how I first saw the Orphanage.

THE WHITE BIRD PASSES

So many things lay in mind. Urgent elusive scraps. The sense of lostness when the train screamed past Loch Na Boune, the last known landmark in Janie's world. Screaming out of time and place altogether. I'm leaving my Mam. I'm leaving my Mam, it had panted. A loud thing in a living hurry. The places it had flashed through focusing in fragments now. Bending boulders like old men groping round a high hill. Dead Man's Bells fleeing whitely from their own wood, shivering down the banks, bowing the train out and past. OYNE in big white letters on a small, black station. A strange name for a place, the only name I remember now. I'm sure I saw it though. Some day I'll go back to see if it's real.

All things seemed unreal to Janie. The dormitory most of all. She looked anxiously over to the chair beside her bed. Her new hat lay safely. So huge that it hid her small bundle of underclothes. She felt her head, still with a small sense of shock, although it had been shaved hours ago, after she left the Courthouse. This morning. Or was it yesterday morning? Time had leapt out of bounds. She lay trying to catch time and return it to its proper place. Its hours eluded her. How enviably Peggy's long hair scattered itself on the pillow there. If I got one wish I'd just ask for all my hair back again. No, I wouldn't. I'd just ask to get home to my Mam again. Not having any hair wouldn't matter if I could just get home again.

But home lay too raw and tender to the piercing touch of thought yet. There was escape from thought in listening to the whispers flitting frighteningly like small bats through the dim dormitory.

"Did you have to read the inscription above the front door, Janie?"

"Yes."

"You've got to remember it by heart as well, though."

"I do. 'Proctor's Orphan Training Home 1891'."

"If ever you don't do your work right, Mrs Thane will take you round to the front door to read it again."

"She makes you say 'training' three times. That's so's you'll never forget."

"And you've got to learn Table Manners off the Card as well, Janie. But you'll get a week to learn them in."

"I've learned a bit of them already:—

I must not talk about my food,
Nor fret if I don't think it good."

"Do you know something, Janie? We get porridge for breakfast every morning except Sundays."

"And we get fish on Sundays. Haddocks. I just can't abide them. You get an egg on Easter Sunday though, Janie."

"And an egg on Christmas morning. Don't forget, Peggy, we get an egg on Christmas morning."

A panic seized Janie and forced her upright in bed:

"When will I get home? I've asked everybody. The Court Man and the Vigilance Officer and Mrs Thane and just everybody. They all let on they don't hear me. But somebody must know *when*?"

"When you're sixteen, most likely." Peggy's casualness distressed Janie. "At least that's when I'm getting home. When I'm sixteen."

"But that's ages!" Janie's distress increased. "That's just years and years. I'm not nine yet. Not till October. I'll have to stay here for eight years."

"Only seven and a half years, Janie," Peggy corrected. "If you're eight and a half now."

"But it's still years and years." Janie was disconsolate. "My Mam could die by that time."

"You can write a letter to her once a month, Janie."

"Mind what you write though. Mrs Thane reads all the letters before they go out."

"I know what I'll do. I'll mark every day off on the calendar till I'm sixteen. It will pass quicker that way."

"That's what I thought when I first came, Janie. Then I just forgot."

"I won't forget." Janie felt very certain. "I'll never forget to count the days off."

"Wheesht! Janie!" Peggy admonished. "The boys' dormitory has gone quiet now. Mrs Thane will be shouting up for silence if we don't go quiet too."

Janie pulled herself down under the sheets, and lay staring for a long time at the changing flecks of colour that always danced into vision when she shut her eyes very tightly. "I won't forget," she thought, staring. "I know fine that I'll never forget to mark the days off."

Chapter Nine

"YOU'RE right lucky, Janie. Leaving and everything." The wistful whispers had echoed enviously through the kitchen all morning.

For eight years, Janie had dreamed of such whispers, troyed within the limited landmarks of Skeyne. And waiting, had forgotten to mark off the days on the calendar. Except, of course, days that had marked themselves off, cutting their inscriptions deeply on the small, memorial cairns of the mind.

How angry Mrs Thane had been when Janie had discovered a "secret" way of commenting on the food. Orphanage Table Etiquette ruled that you must not "talk" about your food. But there was no law against composing "forewarning" chants.

> *Pease brose, Pease brose,*
> *Pease brose again, Chris,*
> *They feed us a' like blackbirds.*
> *And that's a bloody shame, Chris.*

And how annoyed she had been over the desperate postscripts added to the letters home:

"Be sure not to die soon, Mam. Try hard not to get into any fights with Poll and Battleaxe."

"Don't send any more *Love Stories*. Mrs Thane

says they're rubbish. But mind to tell me in your letter when William Corder gets catched and hanged for murdering Maria Marten."

But that was long ago. Janie still added desperate postscripts, but transferred them now to the tail-end of her prayers in the Kirk.

It had taken her longer to learn to part with her dirty underclothes to "the wash" on Monday mornings, and even longer to give up sleeping with her vest and knickers huddled to her in a bundle, because they had smelt homely and personal, an antidote to the sterility of Jeyes' fluid that pervaded the Orphanage.

"I've lost the best chamois, Janie. The new one. The impregnated one for the front windows."

Chris worried into the kitchen:

"She'll go off her head when she finds out. She's at high doh already, all because it's Trustees Day. I was sure I put the chamois into this press with the brooms."

"Stay quiet, Chris," Janie advised with the calm objectivity of the safe onlooker. "Stay awful quiet for a long minute, you'll be able to look for it right when your belly stops heaving up and down."

"You'd better get a start to your front windows." Mrs Thane stalked into the kitchen, dropping through its apprehension like a stone that sent Chris wheeling round and round amongst the brooms.

"What on earth are you rummaging there for, Chris? And it's high time you set off down to the village with the morning milk, Janie! You can take Craig's milk. The shop milk, the police milk. And you'd better take Mrs Mudie's milk too on your first round."

"But Donnie always takes Mrs Mudie's milk now, Mrs Thane. You said . . ."

"I *know* what I said, Janie!" Mrs Thane shot up tall. Her black frock stiffened. The small spots on it leapt out large and white. "I said that if there was a bit of dirt lying anywhere around, you'd be sure to stop and pick it up. I can't spare Donnie this morning. And if you haven't learned yet at your age to close your eyes and ears to improper things, you'll never learn now. Get your coat on, and I'll away and fill your milk pails."

"What's all that about Mrs Mudie's milk?" Chris's curiosity momentarily overcame her anxiety.

"I told you, Chris." Janie's mind had already flown off to a more intriguing tangent. "Mind? About Mrs Mudie having 'the change'. Chris. Chris. Some folk would be a lot nicer if they never wore any clothes at all."

Chris stood shocked into stillness, considering the strangeness of the idea.

"Not everybody," Janie explained incoherently. "Just folk like Nurse Conduit in the School Clinic at the Lane. And the Green Ladies. And the Cruelty Man and Mrs Thane. I once saw her without her frock on. She was rushing to the lavatory. She had bowdie legs, Chris. And black silk knickers. I could have spoken to her about anything when she hadn't her frock on. She just looked ordinary. I bet the School Nurse and the Green Ladies are just ordinary too, when they haven't got their frocks on."

"Haven't you got a start to your front windows yet, Chris? Well, get on with them. Don't stand gaping at me with your mouth open. Your head's in the clouds this morning!"

But Janie knew that Chris was just trying to imagine what lay beneath Mrs Thane's frock.

"And you get going too, Janie. Don't you dawdle down in the village all day either. The Trustees will be here by two o'clock. And mind! No gossiping with Mrs Mudie!"

"High," Skeyne whispered Mrs Mudie was. Though, God knows, other Skeyne women just took "the change" in their stride. Whiles a bit cantankerous right enough. Whiles going clean off their men folk altogether. But never going clean off the Kirk instead and taking to singing dirt or Evangelistic choruses, like orra town's folk at street corners, the way the Mudie wife was doing now. Her that was not only country born, but Auld Kirk bred into the bargain.

Despite that, Janie had missed her morning encounters with Mrs Mudie. They had ceased abruptly one morning when Mrs Thane had inquired about Mrs Mudie's health. And Janie had told her, had just said: "Mrs Mudie's got hot flushes coming all over her, Mrs Thane. And she says she's losing something terrible every month now." Donnie delivered Mrs Mudie's milk after that, leaving Janie with a bewildering sense of disgrace. She had learned over her years in the Orphanage that tact was as important as truth, but had not yet learned to combine them successfully. Nor had she outgrown her affinity with what Grandmother would have called "Ne'er do weels", the Lane "Riff Raff", and Skeyne "Ootlins". Skeyne's word was the best word. The most accurately descriptive. Ootlins. Queer folk who were "oot" and who, perversely enough, never had any desire to be "in".

Entering the low doorway of Mrs Mudie's cottage, Janie always felt the enjoyable apprehension of Gretel entering the Gingerbread House, uncertain whether Witch or Fairy Godmother was in occupation.

Witch this morning. Transforming Mrs Mudie into a tiger dimly pacing the cluttered kitchen. Blind to Janie and the morning milk, but bright and beckoning to her own reflection in the overmantel mirror. Urging it shrilly:

> *There is life for a look at the crucified one.*
> *There is life at this moment for thee.*

The whole room throbbed in dark quick

rhythm with its owner's mood. The grandfather clock gasping the seconds over and past; the kettle hissing on the crook, curled, ready to spring. The dresser still but wary, the saucer eyes of its blue china glinting and watchful.

"Here's your morning milk, Mrs Mudie."

Janie spoke to the face reflected in the mirror. It seemed the realest face. It stared at its own origin, without recognition. Abjuring it in a shrill, high voice:

> Look, Sinner, look
> Unto Him and be saved.

Janie tried to put the milk pail down very quietly. But the table quivered with life too; the milk pail rattled in protest. The face reflected in the mirror went on exhorting, as Janie backed swiftly out through the low door.

> Unto Him who was nailed
> On the tree.

The village had lost all its own livingness since Janie had last looked on it, short seconds ago. Its cottages stood as small and still as the images of themselves, for sale on postcards in Beaton's shop in summer. Or like dolls' houses. Craig's car a toy car now. Craig himself, a tiny tin man at its wheel. Mrs Mudie's garden shot up round Janie's feet. A jungle of boxwood, wild and pungent and bitter. A ladybird, huge and red and clockwork, ticked and hummed across the bewildering box-wood in a blind, mechanical panic.

Fly away home.
Your house is on fire.
Your children all gone.

The sound of her own voice soothed Janie. The childishness of her words shamed her. No wonder Mrs Thane was always puzzling about what was to become of her when she "got out into the world".

Here she was, almost going, and part of her still half believed that ladybirds could interpret and understand. Strange thing, Mrs Thane was either annoyed because, "You're far too knowing for your years, Janie," or anxious because, "You're going to find the world a tough place. I'm sorrier for you than for the other bairns I've brought up."

"You're all behind with your milk this morning, Janie!" Schoolchildren rushed round Leuchar's corner, shouting in their going, "It's gone ten to nine, Janie. You'll be late!"

"None of the Orphanage is coming to School the day," Janie shouted to their retreating backs. "The Trustees are coming. And it's my last Trustees' Day!" Her triumphant words missed their targets vanishing down Barclay's Brae. But the normality of the words set Janie's feet free now. Willing them to carry her out of Mrs Mudie's garden. Out through the village, thinning

120

down into scattered crofts. Out towards the Cairngorms, slinking behind their own protective mists with every step she took in their direction. She could have seen the whole of the world, if the Cairngorms didn't rise immense and blue, shutting Skeyne away from it all.

> O Cairngorms, sae heich and blue
> I'd see the warld
> Were't na for you!

Long ago Janie had thought that if she ran very fast and hidden, along by the side of Leuchar's Wood, she could catch up on the Cairngorms. Rush right into their foothills and take them by surprise, before they had time to hide behind their mists again.

"Aye, Janie. It's a right fine morning."

But no matter how fast she ran nor how hidden her race was, no matter, the Cairngorms were ever swifter, ever more wary, and she had never caught up with them.

"I was saying that it's a fine morning, Janie."

Lower Hempriggs peered over his byre door, his eyes staring out into the fine morning.

"But mebbe your mind's no' on the weather the day at all now, is it?"

"No." Janie reddened under the crofter's twinkling stare. "No. I was thinking about something else."

"Some lad or ither, mebbe?"

"Not that either." Janie's embarrassment increased. "I was just watching the Cairngorms."

Lower Hempriggs turned sidewards and watched the Cairngorms too.

"Aye faith. But they're gey hills, the Cairngorms," he concluded thoughtfully, bringing his keen stare round on Janie's face again. "And so you're just no' for letting on your thoughts at all this morning, Janie?"

"No. Not this morning." Janie laughed herself awkwardly out of reach of the crofter's curiosity, and into the safety of Leuchar's Wood.

"I'm leaving the Orphanage, Mr Tocher!" she shouted back, remembering suddenly. "The Trustees are coming the day. And I'm leaving soon!"

Her shout startled the wood, set all its cushats off on the scold, its insects hurrying on the hum. Janie stood till the hot, scattered haze subsided. And the wood gathered itself together again in still, dark concentration. Listening. Staring absorbed at its own reflection in the loch below.

Two woods there always were, on fine, mist-threatened mornings like this. One stood high and sentinel over Skeyne. The other, down and distant in the loch.

> *Twa woods there was*
> *Before ma een,*
> *But yin lay drooned*
> *In Loch of Skeyne.*

The play of thoughts and words carried Janie to the end of Leuchar's Wood. To where it gave up its own large being with tortuous reluctance. Tearing itself apart and flinging its tattered pieces all over the hill in a blind frenzy. Its remnants rose in sullen copses. Dark and disconsolate.

All else that was broken and rejected by Skeyne lay here too. Crushed beer bottles bejewelled the dump. Jags of emeralds still uncut, glistering through smithereens of crockery, myriad-coloured and many-shaped. Swift and acquiescent to the imagination. The rusted frame of a bicycle rose grotesquely up out of the moss. Rooted there in mounting position, awaiting a strange rider. Some mad man or wise child, to whom the desire could always become the deed.

Lost civilisations had been discovered down under the earth, Janie remembered, as she stood fiercely absorbing the dump. Maybe that's why dumps were always so exciting. Always like coming across some small, lost civilisation too.

"I've found an old world. Older even than the Roman world. What if it *really* was so?"

The largest of Leuchar's copses, the Duck's Wood, dipped down towards the Orphanage. It closed in on Janie. Its waves of near-memory surging up and over her, dark and ice cold!

> *And old worlds red with pain.*
> *And old worlds . . .*

She fixed her mind to the image of the dump, desperately, a drowning man grabbing a drifting flotsam—

And old worlds . . .

For once a poem refused to come to her rescue. Its author, origin and ending eluded her, crying Halt! Only its sparse words rose baldly in the mind:

And old worlds red with pain.

Black with pain. That's what the Duck's Wood was. Ever since the day that Liza had arrived from the Lane, setting the seal of her suffering upon it.

"I thought," Chris had accused, after Liza had gone, "that your Mam was awful bonnie, Janie. You was always telling us that. And I thought it was just my Mam drunk, when she came staggering up the avenue."

"She wasn't drunk!" Janie had defended wildly. "My Mam never never got drunk. She always hated drunk folk. She was just ill, Chris. Awful ill. She had a doctor's line to prove it. I saw it. So did Mrs Thane. You can ask her. My Mam wasn't drunk." Janie brought out the name of Liza's illness triumphantly, completely vindicating the shameful accusation of drunkenness. "She's got an illness called chronic syphilis.

That's what made her stagger. And that's what made her white and not bonnie any more."

But Liza had been beautiful, Janie remembered. Almost like Shelley said. Her beauty made the bright world dim. Not quite the same though. All the other women of the Lane had been grey. Prisoners clamped firmly into the dour pattern of its walls and cobblestones. But Liza had always leapt burnished, out of her surroundings. And in the leaping had made the dim world bright.

Her Mother's changed appearance had shocked Janie into numbness. The Lane, and the dream of returning to it, disintegrated in the wrecked reflection of Liza's face. Dulling in the dimness of her eyes, withdrawing into the pale hollows of her cheeks. Not easily though, nor suddenly. They had sat here in the wood, crouching over the smouldering ashes of old loyalties, trying to coax them into flame again.

"And Poll and Battleaxe and the Duc hess?" Janie had inquired, her question sounding from the voice of a stranger. "How are they all?"

"Fine. Just fine." Liza had cheered at the deceptive narrowing of a gulf. "Aye, asking for you, all of them. Did I mind to tell you that poor old Annie Frigg is dead and gone? She never got over a fall from the top landing to the bottom. One Saturday night with a good shot in. The one and only conscious word Annie ever uttered after that was a swear."

"Did it begin with F, Mam?"

"Aye. It did that."

"I thought that." Janie congratulated her memory with a smile. "That was always the swear that Annie used."

"At least she wasna' a hypocrite." The old Liza, amused and satirical, peeped out for a brief instant. "Not like old Balaclava when she kicked the bucket, cringing and whining to God at the last minutes. Annie, game to the end, went out with a curse. It was gey pitiful though, when you come to think of it. Annie had just been 'saved' again. But I've no doubt that your soul saved is of little comfort till you when your body's sel' is coming to its end. Your soul's a stranger to you, like. But you ken your body's sel' awful well."

"Who got Annie's room, Mam?" An old wonder had prompted the question. The one room in the Lane into which Janie had never penetrated, thereby still retaining its probability of all Annie's bygone promises redeemed.

"None got it." Liza had shattered probability. "And deed it was fit for none when Annie was through with it. We had the Sanitary on the top of us for days. Fumigating and disinfecting. Before any of us could get by her landing without getting knocked down with the stink that come from her room. And that's another thing, Janie." Liza's voice had allowed no period for mourning. "We're all getting new Council houses down by the Cathedral. Another good reason for you coming home again. The Duchess's moving into her house next week. She managed to wangle herself to the top of the list. Her cry aye being the loudest, like. And there was Poll, all set to step into her shoes. All ready to take over the rule of the Lane, when she got a notification about her new house too. Poor Poll. She didna' ken whether to mourn over the loss of power, or rejoice over the acquisition of property. Anyhow it left the road fine and clear for Battleaxe. There's a queer kind of truce in the Lane just now, Janie. Its rulers are no' on speaking terms at all. And their subjects are fair going mad with new freedom. Oh, and you mind on wee Lil? She got the chance of a new house too. She turned it down flat. Said that she would never be able to pass herself amongst a crowd of complete strangers. And that she preferred to stay on in the Lane amongst her old friends. The pathetic thing about that, of course, is that wee Lil hasna' got one friend in the Lane. But she doesna' realise that. And I hadna' the heart to point it out to her. It would have been a real unkindness. Because wee Lil's happier no' realising."

But Liza, who had always realised things, began to realise then that the road back to the Lane was not going to be so easy.

"We'll have a house in the country, Mam. Mind, we always wanted that. With a garden and nasturtiums and a goat. We'll never live in the Lane again. We'll have plenty of money when

I'm educated, you see; that will only be a few years now."

Janie's words lapped against the grey, unseeing rock of Liza's face.

"The Lane will do me fine," she had said bitterly, "for all the time I've got left now."

A vividly remembered fear of death had clutched at Janie's mind.

"You're not going to die, Mam? Not for a long, long time?" She had almost pleaded, "Promise me that you won't die. Just promise this one time." But, knowing now that people couldn't truly make such promises, had sat quietly, filling her eyes and mind with the long lengths of the great trees and shutting out the brooding image of death.

"I'm no' so sure. The doctors dinna' hold out much time for me."

It was then that Liza had groped in her bag for the certificate.

"You can see from that, that I'm gey ill," she had said quietly, proudened by the impression the unfamiliar name of her illness had made on Janie.

"But the doctors can cure you, Mam? Surely they can cure you?"

"I've left it some late for that. They say I need somebody with me all the time now. It's my sight that's failing fastest."

You could pray your intensest prayer ever, stricken by blindness yourself. Your eyes wide

open, staring through the wood without seeing
its trees. And without words at all. Just the heart
beseeching in hurried incoherent beats:

> *O say what it is that thing called light*
> *Which I can ne'er enjoy.*
> *What are the blessings of the sight?*

That had been one of the first poems that Liza
had ever taught Janie on the long road to Grandmother's house. The sudden recollection of it lit
dim corners of her mind, revealing small half-
forgotten things.

All the things I know, she taught me, God.
The good things, I mean. She could make the
cherry trees bloom above Dean's Ford, even when
it was winter. Hidden birds betrayed their names
the instant she heard their song. She gave the
nameless little rivers high hill sources and deep
sea endings. She put a singing seal in Loch Na
Boune and a lament on the long, lonely winds.
She saw a legend in the canna flowers and a
plough amongst the stars. And the times in the
Lane never really mattered, because of the good
times away from it. And I would myself be blind
now, if she had never lent me her eyes.

"And if that Matron gets thrawn about you
coming home, she's got this to contend with."

Liza had waved the doctor's certificate preci-
ously, gently, smiling over it as secretly as if it
had been a magic wand and she only had the
awareness of its power.

But the magic hadn't worked with Mrs Thane. The spell had exploded in the magician's face, confounding the onlookers.

"*That*," Mrs Thane had shot back from Liza, handing the certificate to her, fingertipped, a spill rescued from the flames and still smouldering, "is about the very last reason why Janie should return to live with you again. It is certainly the last reason the Trustees will ever recognise."

Liza had cursed them. Striving for utterance in words that were familiar enough to her ears, but harsh and uneasy on her tongue:

"You smug bastard! You're born, but you're not dead yet! You . . ."

Poll and the others swore slickly. Could say F and B and C smoothly, as if they weren't swears at all, but part and parcel of the Lane's own language. But even ordinary words had always come to life on Liza's tongue. They writhed now through the dim reception room, stabbing it with light each time she swore.

"And God doesna' pay his debts wi' money. But that's something you've still got to learn yet, you . . ."

The fir tree in front of the window closed in on the room. I've never properly heard a swear till now, Janie had marvelled. Mrs Thane hasn't heard one before either. And her face isn't really angry. Not half as angry as it sometimes gets with me for just saying Damn. She just looks fat and lost and bewildered with arrows. The fir tree

130

began to swim in front of Janie's eyes. A great blur of green. "I'm sorry." Her eyes had tried to find Mrs Thane to tell her, "I'm sorry she's swearing at you."

The shame of that day was less now. Janie felt guilty about this. "It should never get less," she protested to herself, "I ought to feel ashamed about it forever and ever."

But the pain of that day remained. My Mam went away without knowing I love her. The words wouldn't come till she was getting on to the bus. And then it was too late.

Unleashed by the desolation of Duck's Wood, Janie raced down into the ordinary world again. Its large brightness rushed upwards to meet her, its fields panted past her, a great haste of green. The Orphanage down in the hollow was the only solid thing in the whirling, sunlit world. It had gathered all its own within it. There was neither sight nor sound of its children.

They'll be polishing the floors like mad. Getting all stickied up. And creaking, every time they rise off their knees.

Janie stopped in her race to enjoy the moments of not having to polish. To recall with apprehension how the house would put out its dark, cold claws and claim her again, catching at her breath with the smell of beeswax, whispering roughly in Scots. And speaking aloud in polite English.

This was true freedom. Out here beyond bees-wax. She shut her eyes to feel the sun groping warmly over her and hotly finding her. You could know an invisible world if you were blind. You could feel its being trembling. Smell its nearness. Hear the thin murmur of its voice.

"You'd better make your feet your friends, Janie! There's a gey bit steer going on down in the house."

The Mannie shouted across from the lythe dyke, slanting above it like a shadow cast by the trees. "They havena' missed me yet, down bye." He nodded towards the house, his felt hat clinging to the back of his head by a miracle. "But they'll have noticed by this time that you're no' there yet, Janie."

The useless ones. A knot of laughter unwound itself, wriggling through Janie in little smiles. Weary Willie and Tired Tim. Ike and Moe. All the funny folk I once knew in the comics. That's us. That's me and the Mannie. Leaning over a dyke in the sun, till a big, fat policeman moves us on with a kick in the pants.

"And I'll warrant you've been on the dawdle again, Janie."

The Mannie unconsciously but severely withdrew himself from the comic strip. And Tired Tim had never been funny, left on his own. Aware of this Janie volunteered seriously:

"Hempriggs is going to scythe his inroads the morn."

"Is he, by God? Did he mention it, like?"

"No. Not exactly. But I noticed. I saw his scythe. He'd been sharpening it. And he was keeping his eye on the weather."

"Mphmmmm." The Mannie turned his eyes towards the weather too. Even the Cairngorms were free of mists now. A small flock of gulls put a cloud in the sky. They watched them dipping and rising and borrowing a sheen from the sun.

"I'm no' so sure about the weather," the Mannie said. "That's the first of them flying inland. From the Brock, likely. There'll be others to follow. I'll warrant it's rough at sea. And we'll land wi' the hinner end of the storm. But mebbe thae chieldies werna' in flight, when Hempriggs took his survey."

"His oats are gey and thin." Janie was enjoying the rare experience of being accepted man to man, in broad Scots, and with authority. "He's got some gey rank-like stuff in yon park."

"And small wonder at it," the Mannie agreed. "Hempriggs should have stuck to concreting. He kens a lot about cement, but deil all about the rotation of crops. And so his corn's shargared, ye think, Janie?"

They stood contemplating the fat, bearded ears of their own corn. Still green over by the Glebe, but yellowing southwards down to Hardhillock.

"I'll maybe mak' a start to the inroads next week, if the storm bypasses us," the Mannie concluded.

133

He'll be a windmill on the hum then, Janie thought, remembering past harvests. Flailing his long arms above the scythe, and singing the hot afternoons over and past.

"This will be your last hairst wi' me then, Janie."

It was just a statement. But, somehow, it needed a reply. An expression of regret.

"I'll miss outside," Janie said truthfully, "I'll miss outside terribly."

The clang of a distant door prevented elaboration. It shot the Mannie up into straightness, and turned his face to Leuchar's Hill.

"I'm taking a turn up bye to look at the gimmers if onybody speirs. And you had best be making tracks for the house, Janie."

Dear Mannie. He was none other than Mrs Thane's husband. But the children had no name for him, other than the Mannie. He hovered on the fringe of Orphanage life. Clumsy, and "in the road" of everybody in the busy kitchen. Ill at ease in the best room. And positively uncomfortable in his stiff, black Sunday suit in the Kirk pew.

His was the shadow that would whiles slope round the back door, wondering "if he could get a bairn or two to give a hand with the tattie lifting?"

The children vied with each other to work for the Mannie. He made slight demands on them, and was so grateful for so little.

"And what's *your* name, lass?" he would inquire with great bewilderment. Never quite sure if the Mannie had really forgotten the name, or if this was a signal for fun, the children would shout protestingly:

"That's Janie! Janie MacVean. She's been here for years and years!"

The Mannie would lowp startled up into the air, knocking over the tattie pails in his surprise.

"God be here! So it is. Of *course* it's Janie. Can ye sing, Janie?"

And without waiting for a reply, would go striding down the furrow, past the children bent double with laughter, singing out of him:

> *There was a wee cooper*
> *Wha lived in Fife*
> *Nicketty. Nacketty. Noo, Noo, Noo.*

Without ever probing, the Mannie knew when any of the children were "in disgrace" with his wife.

"How can ye no' work your work right in the house?" he had once asked Janie, as sadly as if her unhappiness belonged to him too. And the Mannie was the only person to whom she had ever tried to explain it:

"I do try. Truly I do. I start to dust fine, then something comes into my head, and I think about it so long that the time passes, and the dusting isn't done."

Peering over the calves' loose-box, which was momentarily the confessional, Janie had awaited the Mannie's verdict with all the apprehension that sometimes overtook the Kirk on Sunday mornings when the Minister, tired of beseeching God, attacked his congregation with cantankerous cunning: "Can any good thing come out of Nazareth?" That the Minister didn't really want an answer, relieved the doubt on the faces of his congregation. But Janie *had* wanted a reply and, in supplying it, the Mannie had somehow relieved her too.

"The happiest chield ever I kent, Janie, was a chield who hadna' two thoughts to crack between his ears. But God preserve us! Folk couldna' thole to see him so happy about nothing at all. They couldna' comprehend it, ye see. So they just up and lockit him awa'. On the t'ither hand, folk with owre muckle thoughts in their heads, they've been lockit awa' as well. Nothing riles one human being so much as the ither human being that they canna' understand.

"Like the brute beasts, by God! Tak' you a calf that's been born wi' two heads or one leg. That's no' the beastie's wight. It was born that wye, poor vratch. But the ither calves, in the same loose-box, mark you! They'll hound it down and butt it to death. That's the beasts. And whiles human beings are no' muckle better, for all that they've got minds to think things out with. And never comprehending that it's gey ill for some to find the balance, and aye just hell and all to keep it. Do you no' think now that it might be easier to work your thinking in with your other jobbies? It *can* be done, ye ken, Janie. Between you and me and the roan calf there, I do it mysel' all the time."

Janie was vividly to recall and interpret the Mannie's words a short year later: meanwhile they seemed to cover herself and the Mannie with a conspiratorial kind of comfort.

There had always been comfort to the Mannie's being. A smell of dung as coarse and complete as that of the dustbins in the Lane, when you had first lifted their lids. You still sometimes escaped to the fields, just for the smell of him. To gaze on his glorious grime, to hear him sing in the loud uninhibited accents of the causeway:

> *For the Minister kissed the fiddler's wife.*
> *And he couldna' sleep for thinkin' o't.*

The Mannie had set his singing seal on Janie's growing-upness. Had marked the passing of the years with a signature tune. Gently, teasingly at first:

> *For Nancy's hair is yella like gowd.*
> *And her e'en are like the lift, sae blue.*

Now that the gentle preliminaries were over, that skirts were longer, and legs had become a mystery beneath them, the Mannie's song of growing-upness echoed with virility in the early morning byre and in the fields that lay the furthest from the house:

> *O my lass, ye'll get a man.*
> *And syne ye'll need a cradle.*

Furtive, but exciting were his theme songs now. Like the gleam of young girls' thighs once glimpsed in dark corners of the Lane. Mysterious and thrilling and quite unlike the dark, growling sound, "whoring", that the Duchess had applied to it all.

Janie would have got all the blame if the Mannie's songs had ever been overheard. She knew that surely, in the dim, instinctive way that she realised blame had been borne in from some bewildering airt, with her first breath. And, though a sense of blame was ever present, the sins which gave rise to it could not easily be defined, confessed to God, and absolved. God could understand everything, even incoherent guilt, but you were only really sure about this on Sundays. Everybody believed in God on Sundays, then laid Him carefully away with their best clothes for the rest of the week.

Old and forbidding as the Kirk was, it was one of the few places in which Janie's spirit thawed in its narrow cocoon. Bursting out to meet the Word of God according to the prophet Isaiah. Blossoming, as it had blossomed in the Green, to the enchanting sound of far-flung places. Racing through desolate Sharon and Lebanon ashamed. Through Tarshish seas. Up Tyre and into Babylon bloated and bedamned. Down Ephraim and over Idumea.

But the cormorant and the bittern shall possess it; the owl also and the raven shall dwell in it.

And it might have been Leuchar's Hill itself that Isaiah told of, for all that he had ever excited the faces of the congregation, folding their thoughts darkly down into the furrows of their own fields:

God help the poor Israelites if ever they were as deived wi' reiving hoodie craws as we've been over Leuchar's way the year. According to Isaiah there, the bodies of his time had more than their whack of pests and plagues and the like. You would have thought now that such mischances would have quelled the perverse craitturs. But deil the bit o't! Isaiah ranted on of worse to come.

And thorns shall come up in her palaces, nettles and brambles in the fortresses thereof: and it shall be an habitation of dragons, and a court for owls.

Thorns and nettles, by God! Skeyne had known its share of both. Though the Lord in his wisdom had keepit the dragons for the fear of foreign folk in far-off times and places. Knowing, no doubt, that a dragon crawling over the Cairngorms would fair bewilder a decent Skeyne man.

But Isaiah's dragon had never bewildered Janie. It was something she took from the Kirk,

139

a weapon of the imagination which she whiles sent writhing in through the back door, to breathe its fire through the coldness of Mrs Thane's disapproval.

Chapter Ten

THE shrubbery which walled the Orphanage round parted to reveal Mima, the newest Orphan, sitting on the shaft of the wheel-barrow, staring bleakly at the long length of yard which she still had to rake clear of leaves.

"I hate raking this yard." She spoke dully, as if Janie had been standing beside the barrow forever. "It's the hardest of all the jobs in the Orphanage. You never come to the end of it."

That was allowed.

"You finish raking one bit of it"—Mima felt encouraged by the allowance—"then the leaves fall down and you've got to go back and rake it all over again. It's always me that's got to do the raking."

"Because you're the newest. That's why," Janie explained. "That's the job we're all put on to, when we first come here. It teaches you perseverance and self-discipline," she added, echoing Mrs Thane's own words.

But I hated raking the yard too, Janie remembered silently, staring at its grey length and at the treacherous trees and rhododendron bushes that surrounded it. Especially in autumn. I used

to sit on the shaft of the barrow and cry sometimes, because the wind nipped my face all the
time, and the leaves kept whirling down, and it
was like trying to rake the whole of the world
clean, in a wind that had taken a spite to you
and never ended. I was right glad when Donnie
came and I wasn't the newest any more. Because
he had to take over the raking of the yard.

"Never mind, Mima," Janie consoled aloud.
"You'll soon get off the raking now. I'm leaving.
Somebody else will be coming in my place.
They'll be the newest, and you'll get promoted
to another job."

"To running down the village and doing all
the messages?" Mima asked hopefully.

"No. Of course not." Janie guarded her
present privilege jealously. "This is the very last
job you get promoted to. You've got to be old
like me and almost leaving the Orphanage,
before you get to go down to the village amongst
other people. Your next job," she continued
severely, "will just be to scrape the mud off all
the boots in the boiler house. It isn't really a bad
job, Mima," Janie added, touched somewhere
by the desolation on the small girl's face. "I used
to be awfully happy scraping the boots. The
Mannie boils all the hens' tatties in the boiler
house. It's lovely and warm in there in winter.
And he always gives you a hot tattie in its jacket,
when he finds you there. You could," Janie
advised, viewing the stretch of yard still to be

raked, "you could say to Mrs Thane that you've got an awful gripping pain in your belly, Mima."

"But I *have* got a pain in my belly, Janie." Mima looked up wonderingly. "Honest I have. Just here."

"I know." That was accepted. "I sometimes used to get one there too, when I had to rake the yard. Mrs Thane will likely give you a dose of senna though, but it's better than raking. Don't you tell that I mentioned it now. And don't say your belly," Janie warned over her shoulder. "That's vulgar. Mind and just say your stomach!"

The stir had reached its height in the kitchen. That moment when the confusion is so great that nobody cares any more, and everybody is light and hilarious with the burden of caring suddenly gone from them. The mood provided cover for Janie's belated entry.

"You'd better get down to the printing of the place names for the table, Janie." Mrs Thane spoke as if Janie hadn't been away for a long time at all. "Your best printing mind! And write 'The Reverend Mr John McLaren.' Not just plain 'Mr McLaren' the day."

"Yes, Mrs Thane." Relief at not being scolded for lateness made Janie expansive. "I'll print them in two different colours if you like. They'll look extra good in black and red."

The offer was almost accepted.

"But Donnie spilt all the red ink," Alice remembered smugly. "That time when he was doing his graph."

"Yes. And the stain hasn't come out of the desk yet, I see." Mrs Thane examined the desk frowningly. Her finding jolted her out of good humour. "You would all be a sight more careful if you had to pay for all the stuff you waste and destroy. You'll just have to use black ink, Janie. And get on with it now."

The task had a certain prestige. Janie studied the list of Trustees' names with an importance that impressed the children busied with much humbler tasks.

"Is the Head Trustee coming the day, Janie?" Chris peered over Janie's shoulder with suitable deference.

"He's my favourite," Alice admitted, approaching the desk curiously.

"Mine too," Janie agreed. "He's so quiet. He hardly ever says anything. But you've got a feeling that he understands about everything."

"You'll be left behind with them on your own today, Janie. I wouldn't be you for anything."

Donnie's commiseration sparked off a thought in Janie's mind.

"I'm excited in a way about that," she confessed. "I think I'll feel like a real person when I'm alone with them. Not just one of the crowd. And I'm glad because the Dominie went to see

144

the Trustees about preparing me for the University Prelims. I bet they never even knew I was good at lessons, till he told them."

"That's one good thing, Janie," Chris pointed out. "I bet the Dominie didn't tell them one bad thing about you. He's always liked you."

"He might just say one thing that's not too good," Janie admitted. "And he's always saying it to myself, that my essays are the best in the School, but my endings are always sad. And I just can't write happy endings," she explained, "because things don't end that way."

Strange thing that. Janie sat pondering it quietly. You knew the instant you were sad. But happiness always lay either in the past or in the future. I was happy this morning, Janie realised with surprise. About nothing. Just walking along watching the mists steam out from the seams of the Cairngorms. And I know I will be happy when I leave the Orphanage. But I can never pin the actual moment of happiness down in an essay, and recognise it. Saying it is *now*.

The reception room was loud with coughs and nervous with the scraping of chairs. The children in the back row fumbled for the touch of each other's hands and found little reassurance in the contact. They fixed their eyes anywhere, except upon the Trustees' faces. Each trying to find calmness in the contemplation of ordinary things.

But familiarity itself had turned into strangeness. The Wife of the Founder of this Orphanage stared down over everyone from her large canvas above the fireplace, as if she was really seeing them and felt slightly surprised by what she saw.

The Mannie had put on the unease of Sunday with his stiff, black suit, strumming his fingers along the window-sill, tapping his foot in rhythm to a tune heard only by himself.

Mrs Thane was the one person whom the children could see without setting eyes on. Stand erect. Don't stare at your feet. Her warning signals trembled on invisible wave-lengths. Your eyes rested on no particular face, but you were intensely aware of all the faces slanting around you. Most of them familiar. But each of them isolated.

"*Well! Well! Well!* You're to be congratulated, Mrs Thane!"

The small Trustee's greeting riveted all eyes frontwards.

"A fine, healthy crew! A fine, healthy crew indeed!"

The smaller children, not yet familiar with the exuberance of his greetings, stared wide eyed and puzzled, as if he were referring to Sinbad and his Sailors and not to themselves at all. The older children took a sudden, collective interest in the fir trees outside the window, steeling themselves against a fit of the giggles.

If I look at the Mannie now, Janie realised,

turning her face swiftly towards the fir tree too, I know he'll wink. And that will be the end of me for certain.

"And this *can't* be Alice, Mrs Thane! You don't mean to tell me that this is Alice! When you think of the scrap she was."

The children's minds scornfully rejected the small Trustee's assumed ignorance. But their eyes slanted, compelled, in the direction of their unfortunate companion. Groping unwillingly over her. Reluctant to discover Alice enlarged and transformed.

"And. My word! Alick's spectacles certainly improve him."

Alick shot into focus now. Ping Pong. Ping Pong. Ping. And we're coiled up quiet in our inner selves. Pong. And we spring quivering out into a glancing space.

I wish I could change when my turn comes, Janie thought. Into something big enough and strange enough to fit the small Trustee's vision.

"Goodness! Hasn't Donnie shot up in the past year."

If Donnie turned into a giraffe right now, Janie's thoughts raced, the Trustee would get such a surprise that he wouldn't be able to utter another word. The ridiculous thought got out of control, spreading itself grinningly across Janie's face.

Of his bones are coral made . . .
Nothing of him that doth fade.

The lines rushed to Janie's rescue. She steadied her thoughts against them:

> But doth suffer a sea change
> Into something rich and strange.

Her grin wrecked itself on the wide and wonderful phrase. Into something rich and strange. She could look with serious face now at the small Trustee. At Mrs Thane. At all the Trustees. She wouldn't have changed places with one of them. Not for anything. They were all so old. Nothing was ridiculous, or rich, or strange to them any more.

"And Janie? We're going to be losing Janie soon. How many years, Mrs Thane? How long have we had Janie?"

The Head Trustee rose to his feet. The gesture signalled the dismissal of the children, and cut off the flow of the small Trustee's words.

"Stay behind the others," Mrs Thane whispered in Janie's ear. The children filed past her, their small, sidelong glances of awe lengthened her in spirit and in stature. The door closed behind them. Its click separated her from childhood.

"We've had a visit from your Schoolmaster, Janie."

The Head Trustee was speaking long enough for Janie to know the sound of his voice for the first time.

"He tells us you have made excellent progress at school."

"Did you know," Mr McLaren, the Minister, leant forward, cutting Janie from the scene, "that her English papers were the best in Aberdeenshire? Most unusual," he explained, "I read the particular essay. The lifetime of an old woman, complete in a single page. It was difficult to understand how anyone so young could have written it, without having possibly experienced it."

"I didn't realise that Janie was in any way . . ." The small Trustee faltered, his eyes searched Mrs Thane for aid. "I always had the impression that she . . . well, that she . . ."

Mrs Thane came to his rescue.

"She's a puzzle. She can be as crude and knowing as they come. And, at the same time, she's less sophisticated and more sensitive than any of the other children, who haven't had such a deplorable background."

"A disintegrated personality?" the Minister suggested.

"I'm afraid so," the Head Trustee admitted. "That's why this question of further Education presents a problem. The pity is that we sometimes get them too late to adjust the balance."

"How old was Janie when she came to us, Mrs Thane?" The small Trustee put the question.

"Nine. Just on nine."

"Give me a child till it is seven," the small

Trustee deplored. "After that, any one can have it. What's bred in the bone, you know."

"Well! What have you got to say for her, yourself, Mrs Thane?"

The Head Trustee's breeziness drew Janie into their circle again.

"She's honest," Mrs Thane agreed. "She's very good with the younger ones. She's got a nice nature, she never sulks. She's an excellent milker. She can turn out a room well. Indeed, Janie can do anything well when she likes. But she doesn't always . . . like!"

"We're all inclined to be a bit like that, sometimes," the Minister confessed. "It's a very human failing."

"What about an under-housemaid's job for her, Mrs Thane." The small Trustee was struck with the idea and urged it lovingly.

"In some good household you know. Where they'll take an interest in her."

"I'm no' so sure about that," the Mannie intervened for the first time.

"Good, Mr Thane." The small Trustee sounded as if he were aware of the Mannie for the first time, and was anxious to make up for it. "It's excellent to have the practical opinion of a plain man. What would you suggest?"

"If Janie has to go into service at all," the Mannie spoke unperturbed by Mrs Thane's alert attitude, "I suggest that she works at a local farmhouse. She likes outside work. And she's good at it. She'll know where she is, and the folk that she's amongst. At least till she gets another year over her head."

"What do you think, yourself, Janie?" The small Trustee put the question.

Don't fly up. Mrs Thane's eyes pleaded. Don't fly up just now. I tried to prepare you for this.

Janie found the small Trustee's face.

"I don't want to dust and polish," she told it. "And I don't want to work on a farm. I want to write poetry. Great poetry. As great as Shakespeare."

Janie dismissed herself from the room. Surprise rooted Mrs Thane from preventing her. Her last Trustees' Day was over.

There had been no haste about that night's delivery of the milk. No haste at all. It was the last time. And, last times, Janie was gradually beginning to discover, gave you a large sense of freedom. The largeness of the freedom that was over her had diminished the approaching village. World enough until then, Skeyne seemed to have shrunk small and down into the foothills of the Cairngorms. Even the Cairngorms themselves had lost their terrifying immensity.

"I'll be beyond them next week," Janie had thought contemptuously. "I'll know at last what lies beyond the Cairngorms."

The outlying cottages of Skeyne had stood

rooted in tansies, sloping forward as if they had grown up out of the earth itself and were moulded in its slant forever. Women lounged outside their doorways in untidy ease, conscious that the night had a lot of wear in it yet.

"It's yoursel' then, is it, Janie?" Kirsty Withan had peered round her bourtree bush. The fine autumn night had resurrected her.

"For I thought she died long ago." Janie had felt resentful somewhere.

"My faith ye! But ye've shot up, Quean! Ye was just a bairn the other day, when I set eyes on ye! Just a bairn." Kirsty's voice had gabbled urgently. As if it hadn't uttered for years and was deperately making up for lost time. "And how are all the folk up bye at the Orphanage? Old Thane is still to the fore they tell me. Deed aye! Me and Thane will stick them all out yet. We'll see them all in the Kirk yard down bye." She had chuckled as if this triumph was her own and secret. Janie had been glad to escape the old woman's eyes, detaining her with their dumb pleading . . . Speak to me, speak to me, they had urged. I only know that I am truly alive when *other* folk think it . . . Had been glad to strike down through Carron wood to the Orphanage again.

The threshing mill had flung its gaunt grotesque shadow across the corn yard. The mill men had hovered round it like ghosts. Their voices drifting upwards, a dirge in the dusk.

"Roon. Roon. Roon."

"Roon wi' her."

"Roon yet."

"Roon. Roon. Roon."

The younger children, condemned to play outwith the radius of the dangerous mill's shadow, had leapt defiantly in the light. Outcrying the mill men's dirge. Dusk and distance distorting them into little demons, and the words of their familiar game into some weird incantation:

> Queen. Queen
> In paraffin
> Was seventeen
> Caroline.

Losing their otherness only when she had come within hailing distance of them.

"It's Janie! Come on! We can go inside now. We can all go in with Janie. She's big!"

The kitchen at a loss, with the harvest workers huddling inside it. The straws off their boots wisping forlornly across the highly polished floor. The smoke from their pipes curling guiltily upwards. Their great feet scraping in incoherent embarrassment for the coarse, sharny smell of themselves that tussled with the refined but persistent smell of beeswax. Janie, sniffing an aura of battle, had smelt danger. Mrs Thane struck the first blow, opening all the windows with a snap that sent Claystone's voice rushing in to cover the sudden, humble silence.

"Mind you! We've had weeter harvests! A

damned sight weeter! Ye mind on that, Kinmyles? Surely to God ye mind on that? Yon year we were gatherin' in Burnie boozle's corn. By God we were weet! We were baith weet then. Weet up till our verra . . ."

"So you got back at last, Janie!" Mrs Thane's voice had cut into Claystone's recollections with a lash. He had sighed his story back into a silence broken by Kinmyles venturing tentatively:

"I hear that Janie's to be lowsin the sheaves for us, on top o' the mill, the morn."

"Aye. Deed aye!" The Mannie, grateful for some safe and "proper" topic of conversation, had become voluble. "Her first time abune the mill. And her last," he explained. "Janie's going to Kingorm. They've decided to mak' a scholar oot o' her. They have that!"

"Aye, then, Janie?" Kinmyles had said. "So ye'll no' be kennin' ony o' us in a year or twa. They'll be makin a Kingorm lady o' ye!"

"They'll have no need!" Mrs Thane had snapped, straightening up from picking the straws off the floor. "She thinks she's that, already. Kingorm. Kingorm. There's been nothing else in her head or on her tongue but Kingorm, this past week!"

"It's an odd thing about youngsters hereaboots and nooadays," Kinmyles had begun pondering diplomatically, "they all seem to think that the world begins and ends at Kingorm. Though, God knows, I never needed to go further than Skeyne for everything and onything that life has to offer at Kingorm."

"Aye. God knows!" Claystone had agreed banteringly, suddenly forgetful of his austere surroundings. "God knows, Kinmyles! Ye've experienced twa three things that life has to offer at Skeyne. God aye, Man! Ye could just tell a gay story, if aince ye get crackin'."

"Cry the mill men in for their supper, Janie!" Mrs Thane's command had prevented such an exciting possibility. "Run on, now! You'll get yours when they're finished."

"So the brose is up, then, isn't, Janie?" The mill men had emerged in a cloud of dust from the dark mysterious caverns of the mill. Shaking themselves and straightening up into livingness.

"You're to be lowsin' the sheaves till's the morn, Quean?"

"Keep an eye on auld Hughie here, then! He's an auld man, Janie! But he's no' short o' young ideas. He'll hae ye coupit down in the mill, head first!"

Their words had struck and faded.

"She'll be a fine change fae auld Maggie Hooch!"

"Nothing the maitter wi' auld Maggie Hooch!"

"Damn all the maitter wi' her, Dod. Except auld age."

"An ill enough thing, auld age!"

"It's fairly that! It's a thing ye can do nothing wi'!"

"Such as, Dod? Come on now, Man! Dinna be shy. Out with it!"

Their laughter had belched upwards. The dusk had questioned it quiveringly, then dismissed it. But Janie had stood holding on to it. Holding on to her awareness of the possession of her body. She had been aware of it before, had glimpsed it in the smirks of the boys at school, had overheard it in their whispers. A mild awareness. But grown men were beginning to acknowledge it now. There was something cruel and fierce in their knowing.

The Cairngorms had begun to close in and were pressing down on the howe. Carron wood had crept upwards till its trees stood rooted against the sky. Silence had circled all the landscape, and held it trembling prisoner. A peesie had cried through the silence, weeping its grief across the stubble field. Some long, long grief that had found an echo in Janie herself. Her pain became submerged in the peesie's cry. Herself and the landscape had stood in some ache, waiting for release.

> *Guard us, we pray*
> *Throughout the coming night.*

It was then that she realised why the Minister always chose that hymn to end the Evening Service. Because the aloneness of night was beyond the bearing of the land itself. It caught you, the land did, if you walked it at night. Held you hostage. Clamped and small within its own im-

mensity, and cast all the burden of its own aloneness upon you.

The wind had begun to threaten the air.
Passionately she had longed for the wind to come.
To blow herself and the landscape sky high into
movement and coherence again. Almost she had
been aware of the wind's near fierceness. Ready
to plunge the furious hillside burns down into
Cladda river. To hurl the straws over all the
dykes. To toss the chaff into the eyes of the pro-
testing people, bending before it, flapping in their
clothes like scarecrows. To sting the trees in
Carron wood into hissing rebellion. To give the
land some loud, loud cry, other than that of pain.

"Aye. But the wind's hoverin'. She's goin' to
rise."

The mill men were clanking out now. Pausing
by the back door. Sniffing the night.

"Think ye that, then, Dod?"

"I wouldna' wonder at it. We could do wi' a
breesie o' wind to dry out the stooks."

"A breesie, man! No' a bloody gale, though!
And that's what's in it. She's on the road! A
muckle North-Easter!"

They had dragged themselves reluctantly away
from the contemplation of the night.

"Well then, Janie! This time the morn's night,
Quean, ilka bone in your body will be hippit,
after a day at the mill!"

"God aye, Janie! You'll feel that sore, ye'll
have to lie on your belly!"

"Never mind, Janie! The first day at the threshing mill is aye the worst day."

"To say nothing of the yavins. They'll have ye itchin' a' night. Belly and all!"

"Coarse things, yavins, Janie! Ye ken the cure for them, though, Quean?"

"Hardly, hardly, Dod, Janie has never lowsed on the mill before."

"Ye tell her, then, Jeems! Ye ken all the answers!"

"Na, hardly. I dinna' like."

"All right! I'll tell her masel! It's like this, Janie. Ye tak' off all your clothes. Sark and all. No cheating. And shak' yoursel' in front o' the fire. Just mind that auld Hughie here doesna' nip up bye for a wee peep when you're doin't."

Their laughter had shaken the darkness again. They had carried their joke with them, along the stubble field.

"She's risin' already! We're in for a gale the morn, right enough. You'll need your goggles on the mill, Hughie. The chaff will fair blind ye!"

"Never him! Never Hughie! He likes to wink to a bonnie lowser wi' his bare e'en. That so, Hughie."

"Na, na. Na faith ye! Janie's just some young for winkin' to yet!"

"Janie! Janie!" The Mannie's voice had assailed the sky. "Janie! Where have ye got till?"

"She's no' that young." The mill men began to

laugh amongst themselves. "Harken till auld Thane cryin' awa' there. She's old enough for him to be anxious, now. She'll soon be ready for the knife."

"Janie! O, there ye are! Where are the ithers? Chris! Alice! Donnie! Come on in, now. Come on! The hale jing bang o' ye! Come on awa' in . . ."

Also by Jessie Kesson

ANOTHER TIME, ANOTHER PLACE

'Miss Kesson writes beautifully, her strong, delicate prose full of poetry and humour'
– *Selina Hastings, Daily Telegraph*

In 1944 Italian prisoners of war are billeted in a tiny village in the far northeast of Scotland. Janie, who works the land and is married to a farm labourer fifteen years older than herself, is to look after three of them. While her neighbours regard the Italians with a mixture of resentment and indifference, Janie is intrigued by this glimpse of another, more romantic world – with almost inevitable consequences. Much more than a simple love story, *Another Time, Another Place* is also a vibrant portrait of a rural community enveloped by an untamed landscape.

THE VICAR'S DAUGHTER
By E. H. Young

'She brought a shining truthfulness to her observation of ordinary, or seemingly ordinary, personal relationships; she had gaiety and a rich fund of subtle and delicately astringent humour' – *The Times*

The Reverend Maurice Roper awaits his cousins' return to Old Framling with a mixture of desire and dread: years have passed since he saw Edward, his childhood hero, and Margaret, the woman he secretly loved, but whom Edward married. As temporary incumbent of the parish, Maurice has taken only one decisive step. Although he is reluctant to acknowledge how deeply past slights and thwarted desire still rule him, he is yet aware that his action could disrupt forever the household he so envies. Here, with her characteristic piquancy, E. H. Young explores the pain of loving – and of being unloved – to produce an evocative account of human frailty.

BLAMING
By Elizabeth Taylor

'One of our foremost novelists' – *Angus Wilson*

In this her last novel, published a year after her death, Elizabeth Taylor, with a scrutiny that is at once compassionate and devastating, examines blaming – of oneself, of circumstances, of others.

When Amy's husband dies on holiday, she is supported by Martha, a young American novelist whose acquaintance Amy is ungratefully reluctant to maintain on their return to England. But the skeins of their existence seem inextricably linked, as grief gives way to resilience and again to tragedy. Reversals of fortune and a compelling cast of characters, including Ernie, ex-sailor turned housekeeper, and Amy's wonderfully precocious granddaughters, add spice to a novel that delights even as it unveils uncomfortable emotions.